PRAISE FOR CB SAMET

Four-time award winning author

"Samet's prose vacillates skillfully between various registers, expressing sensuality, suspense, and humor, as needed."

— KIRKUS REVIEW (ON ROMANCING THE
SPIRIT SERIES BOOKS 1-6)

MASTERS FILE: 2018 Readers' Favorite Honorable Mention in Romantic Suspense category

CHRISTMAS COLLECTION
THREE MAGICAL ROMANTIC SUSPENSE NOVELLAS

CB SAMET

CHRISTMAS COLLECTION

CB SAMET

HOLLY'S HOLIDAY

Gregarious Holly and her mischievous ghost elf set out to match-make the town's newest single addition for the holidays. But when they force Drex's secret as a former spy to light, looming danger closes in on them. Can Holly and Drex save Christmas and each other?

CHAPTER 1

Drex sat down on the park bench. "African swallow or European swallow?"

"Doesn't matter. A swallow cannot carry a coconut." The man beside him on the bench pushed his glasses up on his nose as he shifted his weight in the chair. Ludvik's English was good for never having lived outside the Czech Republic.

"I divided information. Some on phone and some on USB," Ludvik said.

Drex withdrew his phone and laid it on his thigh. The man did the same.

As the data transferred, Ludvik dabbed a handkerchief to his forehead, despite the cool air around them. "When do I get immunity?"

"The information needs to be verified, and then the US government will be in touch."

"You're not the US government?" Ludvik's voice raised an octave in surprise.

"I'm just the middleman." Drex kept his gaze scanning

his surroundings—Letná Park was beautiful despite the bare trees of November. A pale blue sky held wisps of white clouds. A breeze dropped the wind chill to around forty degrees. Birds flocked near picnic tables in search of bits of crumbs on the ground. As nervous as the informant was, he didn't seem to notice his beautiful surroundings.

"I also have instructions about getting my family to safety." Ludvik withdrew a manilla envelope.

Drex glanced down at the data transfer between phones. Seventy-five percent complete. "I don't handle that part."

"Please." He pushed the envelope toward him.

Drex's role was information transfer. If this informant was brokering a deal for immunity for himself or his family, then the CIA needed that information—not him. He wondered if the informant would hold back on the rest of the information if his terms weren't met.

"My job—" Drex started to say gently, but a shot rang out, and the informant's head snapped back.

Sniper.

Instinct kicked in, and Drex dove over the back of the bench. He sprinted for cover as pedestrians in the park screamed. His heart thudded, waiting for the second shot intended for him. It didn't come. Whether that was due to obstructing trees or an unwillingness to accidentally hit a civilian, he didn't know.

The shot had probably originated from the Hanavský Pavilion, since the iconic structure gave a panoramic view of the park from the peak. Drex didn't have time to investigate.

Even as he ran and his mind calculated an escape route, he wondered who the shooter could be. Was it someone from the informant's government, the US government, or a third party? And who had discovered their clandestine meeting? The only people who'd known were the two of them and the agency where Drex worked.

Two blocks from the shooting, he caught up with a crowd of tourists walking outside Kouzlo Museum. He slowed to join them—blending in for a few minutes and controlling his breathing so as not to draw attention to himself. He scanned his surroundings for anyone after him as he tugged a baseball cap out of his pocket and pulled it on.

Two men were on the hunt, necks snapping different directions as they searched. Humpty and Dumpty wore black cargo pants, black leather jackets, and intense, scowling expressions. Drex didn't know them or who they worked for, but they were certainly trouble.

When the crowd moved to enter the museum, Drex cut across Valdstejnska Road and through a forecourt on the way to the metro station.

As he continued underground, he pulled out his phone and speed dialed a number. "Chester. Code Brown," he said.

"Oh, no! You about to be rolled up? Are you okay?" the woman asked.

Code Brown was their alert that they'd been played— literally when crap hit the fan. Some type of double-cross was happening, and they needed to cut and run. *Rolled up* was spy code for discovered and captured. Hopefully he wouldn't be, but he'd never been so close to being ensnared before today. He felt like death itself was breathing down his neck.

"I'm working my exit strategy. I'm okay, but this is serious."

"Zielinski?" Chester asked.

Sandra Chester, a feisty black woman in her sixties, had been Drex's assistant since he'd joined Zielinski's team. All of the team worked remotely, so he'd only seen her the few times Zielinski had wanted video conference calls, but they talked several times a week amidst the planning and execution of missions.

"Could be." Drex worked to slow his breathing as he rummaged through tickets—he'd pre-purchased one for the bus, one for the tram, and one for the subway. "Only the three of us knew where the drop would be."

He preferred to cultivate prospective informants himself and build the relationship before acquiring whatever secrets they had, but Drex had stepped into this delivery cold, never having met Ludvik before today. High-risk information exchanges like this were better done *not* in person, but apparently this defector wouldn't hear of it. Based on the bullet through his head, he hadn't made a wise decision.

"You've got your arrangements?" Drex asked his handler after scanning his card and entering the boarding platform.

Despite never meeting face-to-face, he'd bonded with her over the last seven years. Forming attachments in his line of work created an occupational hazard, but he trusted Chester with his life. She'd helped him out of many tough spots and had an uncanny ability to forewarn of danger.

"California will be lovely this time of year," she said.

She wasn't moving to California, and he would never know her exact relocation spot. He hoped it would be somewhere tropical. Jamaica perhaps. She deserved it.

"You have any guidance for me?" he asked.

"The spirits are telling me you should pick B."

He'd never known what to make of Chester's claim to interact with spirits, but he thought of her gift as intuition rather than something other-worldly. And he wholeheartedly trusted Chester's intuition; it had saved him from more than one tight spot.

Option B.

He had five different identities ready for five different cities as contingency plans should something run afoul. While Chester had helped him set up the identities, she didn't know which letter corresponded to which location. In this way, she could never be forced to surrender information about his new life.

Hopefully, she would arrive safely at the tropical paradise destination he envisioned for her and never have to contend with the fallout from this debacle.

"Thank you for everything." He needed to wrap up the conversation before he lost his cell signal as he stepped onto the train.

"Easy now," Chester said in a sweet, soothing tone. "This doesn't mean goodbye forever. Just for a bit."

"Oh, yeah? Your demons tell you that?" he teased.

She gave him a cluck of disapproval. "Spirits. Not demons."

"Stay safe." He looked down at the envelope in his hand from the defector. Ludvik's dying request.

"You enjoy your next adventure." She disconnected the call.

Next adventure? All he planned to do was lay low and keep his head down. He had no way of knowing if the sniper was from his team, the Czech government, or the CIA. All of these groups would now be after him—either because they wanted the information he now had or because they thought Drex was the traitor.

HOLLY PULLED her office door shut and locked it. She adjusted the hanging green and red wreath. Delightfully warm with Christmas spirit, she barely noticed the biting cold wind. After adjusting her hat and scarf, she practically skipped down the sidewalk.

Tonight was the night. Tonight, Figgy would appear, and for the next twelve days, the two of them would spread Christmas cheer.

She walked the few blocks home, grateful the sidewalk had been cleared. Her exterior Christmas lights blinked white, green, and red. She'd decorated her front door to look like a slender, gift-wrapped present. Too bad the inside of her house wasn't as picturesque as the outside— or at least the outside night view, since daylight revealed peeling paint and tattered shingles.

After unlocking the door, she let herself inside and dropped her keys and purse in the foyer. To the left, her Christmas tree twinkled in the unfinished living room. To her right, the kitchen smelled of paint sealant. At least she had heat.

She'd purchased the older home as a foreclosure. The foundation was in good condition, but everything else was outdated—from the dark wood paneling in the living room to the bland kitchen cabinets to the faded wallpaper in the bathrooms.

Nothing a little TLC couldn't fix—except that the projects seemed never-ending. When she wasn't busy buying and selling homes for her clients, she poured blood, sweat, and tears into her own. Yes, all three of those ingredients from her body had gone into this house.

She hung up her coat in the closet and walked toward the living room fireplace. Could she get the flue working in time to enjoy a fire this Christmas?

Lifting the peppermint scented candle from the mantle, she inhaled the fragrance. She would forever be instantly filled with happiness and fond memories at the smell of peppermint. After setting it back down, she used the lighter beside it to set the wick to flame.

December 12th.

She would let the candle burn tonight—and tomorrow, Figgy McJingles would arrive.

Victor Zielinski bit off the end of his cigar and spit it into the trash can. After lighting it, he leaned back in his chair and puffed.

He didn't like loose ends, and Drex Alister was a loose end. The operation was supposed to flow smoothly—once the Czech made the exchange, he died then Drex died. His men had been instructed to then remove all sensitive information from the informant and the spy. Instead, Drex ran, and they'd been forced to chase him, hoping to apprehend him as a traitor.

He'd escaped—with the envelope.

"Victor? Are you still there?"

"I'm here," he grumbled.

"What are you going to do about Alister?" Donna repeated. As the Associate Deputy Director for Intelligence, she was only a few positions below the Deputy Director of the US Central Intelligence Agency.

Zielinski took a long, slow drag on his cigar and blew out smoke. "He's out of my organization." What more did they want? He was a burned spy who would go into hiding—already had by all accounts. "You saw the video. They made the exchange, and then Alister had his sniper take out the defector." Zielinski had paid one of his own to record the encounter. He'd watched the video first in case it needed doctoring, but it hadn't. Events were clear: the exchange took place as the Czech—Ludvik—passed off the manilla envelope, and then he was shot.

"They didn't make the exchange," Donna said.

"What?" Zielinski sat up straighter.

"I'm not sure what was in the manila envelope, but Ludvik still had possession of the jump drive when Czech authorities found him. We were able to confiscate it from police evidence."

Zielinski's mind raced with how to spin this. "Drex must have thought the information was in the envelope and gave the kill signal. What was in the envelope?"

"We don't know."

"Are you going after Drex Alister?" he asked.

"We need answers."

He cursed silently. That was a "yes." And if they captured Drex, could Zielinski's involvement in the hit come to light? Drex couldn't possibly have any proof, but the cunning ex-spy could try to find evidence in the time it took the CIA to close in on him. And he probably had Sandra Chester on his side. His savvy handler had disappeared at the same time Drex was burned—a tell-tale sign of where her true loyalty resided.

"There is another conundrum," Donna said.

He grimaced and reached for his drawer. Antacid or bourbon? They were side by side in his desk. Based on the familiar burning in his gut, he reached for the antacid.

"What's the conundrum?" he asked casually, keeping his voice even.

"Alister helped Ludvik's family out of the country."

"To where?"

"We don't know. They've vanished as well. What traitor takes the time and risk to move his informant's family?"

"It was probably his best way out of the country. You and the Czech government are hunting one man, and he escapes by posing as the husband and father to the family sneaking out with him."

"Perhaps."

He hadn't convinced Donna because his argument was thin. Drex would be faster and more mobile without someone's family to look after. Why had he done that?

Guilty conscience that he'd somehow been responsible for Ludvik's death?

"Be careful," Zielinski warned. "Drex Alister is the deadliest contract spy I've ever trained," he lied. He hadn't trained him, and he had no idea if Drex was deadly.

His operatives possessed a range of cultivated skills, but they were in the business of information exchange, not murder or assassination. If someone died by their hand, it would more than likely be self-defense. As far as Zielinski knew, Drex had never killed anyone.

The CIA didn't need to know that.

"We'll proceed with caution," Donna assured him.

So will I, Zielinski thought.

He took a swig of bourbon to chase down the chalky taste of the antacid. He suspected that if Drex discovered the CIA was after him, he would want to clear his name rather than go to ground like a well-behaved dog. He couldn't risk Drex digging up Zielinski's buried bones of evidence and the money trail proving he'd been paid to eliminate Ludvik.

CHAPTER 2

*H*olly woke at five am and tossed her covers aside. After standing and stretching, she adjusted her Christmas tree print cotton pajamas. Today would be glorious.

"Figgy?"

When she didn't receive a reply, she dressed quickly, pulling on blue jeans and a long-sleeve shirt with a sequined candy cane on the front. She bounded down the stairs, careful to avoid the loose board, fourth from the bottom, and not grab the insecure railing. The stairs were one of many items on her house repair to do list.

"Figgy?" She went to the kitchen but didn't see him there.

In the living room, near the tree, she spotted him scrutinizing her decorative efforts. He was about four-feet tall but hovered a foot off the ground. He had a full head of wavy brown hair, punctuated on either side by plastic, pointy elf ears. His outfit was classic commercial elf apparel—green vest over a red shirt with flared collar, red leggings, green pointed shoes, and green and red striped hat with a golden bell on the end. The most startling part of his appearance was the way his whole body shimmered with semi-transparency.

"Merry Christmas," she said.

He turned around at her words and smiled at her. "There burning on the mantle / you remembered to light the candle." His face was young—maybe eight or ten years old—with rosy cheeks. Despite his appearance, he acted much older.

"Of course." She returned the smile. "'Tis the season." She'd bought the magical peppermint candle at an estate auction three years ago. The instructions pasted to the bottom advised lighting the candle December twelfth and letting it burn past midnight.

On a whim, she'd done so and woke to find the ghost in her house. He'd been dressed to look like an elf then as well. She'd initially panicked, blew out the candle, and ran outside of her apartment of the time. When she'd returned home, he was still there. She'd visited the local family doctor—Charles Akers—and had him run tests under the auspices she was experiencing concerning headaches. Blood work and brain imaging had been unrevealing—no brain tumor, no electrolyte abnormalities, no hormonal imbalances. After accumulating those medical bills, she'd underwent sessions with Candy—now Candy Akers—the town councilor. Stress relief sessions hadn't made the elf disappear.

Despondent, Holly had returned to her apartment and addressed the ghost directly.

"Why are you here?"

"To bring Christmas cheer!"

"What are you?"

He'd looked down at his attire and back up at her. Gesturing to his outfit, he'd said, "You need more of a clue?"

"You look like an elf, but you also look like a ghost."

He beamed. "I am both. To spread joy / I am your host."

"Do you always rhyme?"

"Would you prefer I mime?" He extended his arms and flattened his palms before moving them up and down as if against an invisible wall.

Holly had laughed. Whatever this creature was, he clearly posed no threat to her. After that, they'd exchanged introductions, and he explained he would be visible only to her—*whomsoever lighteth the candle / shall take command of my handle*—until December twenty-fifth. She was allowed his services for that duration to embark on any activity that would spread joy and cheer.

"What delights await?" Figgy's words brought her back to the present and her work-in-progress home. "New couples to create?"

"I have a few ideas." She gave a mischievous grin.

"What of your fate?"

"Me? I'm happiest when I'm bringing people together."

Last year, they had paired the Akers together through careful planning. Figgy had a knack for knowing when and where people would be around town. His uncanny ability paired with Holly's intuition about what people liked and who they may be compatible with made them a dynamite duo in connecting future couples.

Figgy said, "But your blonde hair glows in the sunlight / And your blue eyes are ocean bright."

She put her hands on her hips. "Flattery? What's gotten into you?"

"You could find your man / We only need to plan." He blinked big, brown eyes at her.

Holly frowned. Her Christmas elf had never been this persistent about her own love life. She'd trusted a man once; she wasn't ready to do so again.

Playing matchmaking for others was satisfying enough, and she had the added insight of Figgy's supernatural abilities to know the couples they paired would be safe together—such knowledge hadn't been available to her during her own relationship.

DREX LET himself into his new house. He'd never been a homeowner, but if he was going to blend in to small town USA, he needed a cozy four-bedroom house like this. The walls were bare, but the essential furniture was present—kitchen table, living room sofa, bed and dresser in the master, refrigerator, washer/dryer, and treadmill.

He set his briefcase and house keys on the kitchen table beside a gift basket of chocolate, nuts, and fruit.

He read the note:

Congratulations on your new home! Thanks for using Holly Realtors.

Yours Truly, Holly Sanders

Drex scowled. His first order of business would be to

get her to drop the key she had in his mailbox. He couldn't have a realtor coming and going as she pleased.

His mobile phone rang. "Hello, Chester." The incoming number was unregistered, but she was the only person who knew his new phone number.

"How's your new home?"

He shook his head in disbelief. Of course, she knew he'd arrived today. "Nice. I managed to do ninety percent of the search and purchase remotely." Fortunately, he'd never had to meet this Holly Sanders face-to-face. She was entirely too enthusiastic about her job and asked too many questions.

He'd found the house online and made an offer electronically. Instead of immediately accepting the offer as the representing realtor, Holly Sanders had requested a phone call to discuss the purchase. She'd been more interested in making sure the house was the right fit rather than making fast money.

"Do you have kids?" she'd asked.

"Is that relevant?"

"Of course it is." Her voice was a fountain of cheer. "You want to be in the right public-school district."

"No kids."

"What about physical activity?"

"Excuse me?"

"There's a gym near the house you picked out, but I know a subdivision closer to biking and trails and another near a golf course."

He frowned. "No golf. The house I picked will be fine."

"Where will you be working? Let's make sure the traffic patterns are favorable for your commute."

"Blitzen is a small town. I'm not worried about traffic patterns. I want *this* house." How was he to get her to stop probing? Perhaps the prospect of more money. "And I'd like to pay your company to add basic furniture and appliances."

"Do you want to send me some color schemes and designs you might like?"

"No." The thought of looking at color palettes had had him rubbing his temple. "Just keep it functional. No frills."

"No frills. Got it. Will you be needing lawn equipment, too?"

Lawn. He would be a homeowner and a *lawn* owner. The image of himself pushing a mower seemed serenely domestic. After a hot day of yardwork, he could relax on the porch with a cold beer. But lawn mowing days wouldn't arrive until the spring, and he would first have to survive until then.

"No lawn equipment," he'd answered Holly. "But I would like a treadmill."

Drex spotted the treadmill in one of the spare bedrooms as he pulled his attention back to the conversation with Chester.

"How is your new place?" he asked her.

"Sunny and warm."

He snorted. That probably meant she'd moved to Alaska.

"Did you give yourself an equally ridiculous alias?" He'd been stupefied after the incident in Letná Park when he pulled out his new passport and driver's license only to discover his name was Chris Holiday.

"You like it?"

"I'm surprised you didn't just pull out all the stops and make my last name Kringle. Did you know I'd be embarking this identity in December?" He wasn't going to also tell her the name of the town he now lived in was the same as one of Santa's reindeer. Chris Holiday moved to a town named Blitzen in December and had purchased his house from a woman named Holly.

Ridiculous.

"Could be a spirit told me." Her tone was filled with amusement.

"Could be you're mocking me."

"I would never," Chester said, her voice dripping with honey.

"Look, Chester." He sat in his recliner and leaned back. "I'm grateful for all of your help—going all the way back to when we started together. I hate that our friendship burned you."

"You're good people, Drex. I knew that from the first case I assisted you on."

"Oh, yeah?"

"You were neck deep in the new Irish Republican Army trying to turn Finnegan. He wasn't budging, even as you learned about the bombs placed around Waterloo and Heathrow. You had a choice to make—out your cover and stop the immediate threat or let a few civilians die from the bombs but stop thousands of deaths later by staying under cover and learning all the players and their hide-outs. You managed to do stop the bombs and turn Finnegan."

Drex's mouth went dry and his head spun. "How did you know about the bombs?" He'd written in his report that Finnegan had stopped the bombs, hoping to grease the wheels for better treatment of him by the British government as they learned his secrets. Only he and Finnegan knew Drex had sequentially deactivated the bombs after he'd restrained Finnegan. It had taken giving Finnegan an ultimatum to turn him—go willingly and cooperate, or the government would likely force the information from him. Drex's cover ended with that, but he'd accomplished his mission.

"I've told you before—the spirits speak to me. Anyway, after that mission, my loyalty lay with you. I knew you'd always find a way to do the right thing and not sacrifice others for personal gain. Now," she continued, "why don't you take your new town and your new name as a sign that you need to enjoy the month? Soak in the season in whatever city you landed in and immerse in the Christmas spirit."

"Christmas is for suckers," he grumbled, only half joking. Besides, he had work to do in order to figure out how to clear his name. Although he had a new home and new identity, he wasn't under the misconception he was safe. It was only a matter of time before either Zielinski or the CIA caught up to him.

Chester let out a harrumph. "Hogwash. Just because you never had a family to show you the meaning of Christmas doesn't mean it's without significance. Keep an open mind—and an open heart—and you might be surprised what's possible."

"I don't have time for distractions. But if it means that much to you, I wish *you* a Merry Christmas."

"It's a start."

❄

WHEN HOLLY WALKED into the kitchen to make breakfast, Figgy followed.

She filled her blender with ice and added almond milk and powdered kale-protein mix. "I was thinking about a few of our bachelorettes. There's Hope, the interior decorator, Linda, the dentist, and Regina, at the bakery. As for our bachelors, we have Rick the lawyer and Chance—he runs the town's meals-on-wheels company."

Figgy cocked his head to one side. "Someone's new this holiday / someone's come from far away."

Holly blended her breakfast as she considered the elf's rhyme. Someone new from far away?

"Oh!" She poured the green mixture into a tall glass. "I sold a house last month to someone new. Chris Holiday. He was not very personable over the phone—especially for someone with that name. I've no idea what he looks like or if a relationship with one of these women is possible. He's Regina's age though—mid-thirties—so there's potential. She runs the bakery with her mom, Janet." Tapping a finger on her chin, she considered the match. She didn't have enough information about Mr. Holiday.

After a long drink of her shake, she said. "I need to meet him. I need to size him up and see if he's worthy. She's super sweet, which might melt his icy first impression. I can drop by as his realtor and welcome him to the town."

"Go to the bistro at ten / you'll meet your mystery man again."

"Again?" she headed back upstairs to her bedroom,

shake in hand as she calculated the time she could take to exercise and work a bit on the house before going to the bistro. "I haven't actually met him yet—we've only talked over the phone."

Mystery man was right. And she would learn more about him and see if she and Figgy could work their match-making magic.

CHAPTER 3

$\mathcal{D}$rex drove to the grocery store and found a parking spot near the cart repository. Last night, he'd snacked out of the basket his realtor had left for him as he reviewed everything he knew about Ludvik's case, but now he needed real sustenance.

After grabbing a cart, he headed inside and worked his way aisle by aisle since he wasn't familiar with the layout. He loaded his cart with cleaning supplies, laundry detergent, brooms, and a mop. As he scanned the shelves, he thought of how he'd have to take into consideration things like air filter sizes and light bulb wattage.

He tried to gauge how he felt about domestication. He could certainly manage it for a few months and may even enjoy it. He'd already decided that if he survived long enough to clear his reputation, he wouldn't go back into the spy business. The lies and deception were tolerable—until it cost a man his life. And the prospect that the guilty party might have originated from Drex's organization only further soured his taste for the business.

But could he follow his dreams?

He added canned soups to his cart as he pulled out a worn postcard from his pocket. He'd bought it at a convenience store in San Francisco, but the "where" wasn't important. The "what" mattered.

The photo was a picturesque bookstore front, though a little large. Through the window display, he could see crumpled shelves of colorful books under soft golden light. He tucked the picture back in his pocket. He'd imagined something similar, except in small town America with large window storefronts under colorful eaves.

"They're not ripe yet."

Drex's attention snapped back to the present where he stood in the produce section, avocado in hand. He assessed the man before him who'd spoken—early sixties, barrel chested, white hair, and a slight curve of his lips that offered the possibility of friendliness, unless it was a ruse to lull someone into a false sense of security. No gun and no place to conceal one in his jeans and flannel shirt. Threat level was to-be-determined.

The white-bearded man picked up an avocado. "They'll need a few more days. You'll know they're ripe when they're a darker color and a bit softer."

Drex filled a bag with three of them. "Thanks for the advice."

The man wasn't wearing a name tag or store apron, so why was he dishing out advice about perishables?

"Are you visiting for the holidays or settling in?" He reached up and stroked his white beard.

Drex's mind honed tighter at the way this man had scrutinized his cart, his appearance, and the absence of a wedding ring. He'd assessed Drex the way Drex assessed everyone. He was probing for Drex's intentions.

Then, he realized he knew this face. Drex had done his research online about the small town, and this man was the town sheriff—his appearance looked different, owing to the long beard he currently sported, whereas his online photo was smooth skin on his square jaw.

Drex weighed his options in a millisecond. He was seen with a cart of cleaning supplies no visiting tourist would be purchasing. His usual reply if a stranger interacted with him was to keep the interaction punctual and move along—safer for everyone because someone watching might mistake the bystander as a person of significance to Drex. Plus, he rarely stayed in a city for more than a few days unless he was building rapport with an informant to acquire secrets, so there weren't repercussions for being unfriendly to strangers. In this town though, he needed to blend in, which would require him to be congenial—especially to law enforcement.

"Settling in," Drex replied, plastering a friendly smile on his face.

"Tough time of year to move," the man added. "Starting new during the most social season of the year?"

"Yeah," he gave a light chuckle. "I'll have some adjusting to do."

A brunette walked past, pushing her cart and waving. "Hi, Sheriff Carpenter."

Drex's jaw clamped as he tried to maintain the smile—his suspicion confirmed. The first person he met in his new life was the town sheriff? Unbelievable.

The sheriff extended a hand. "Joe Carpenter."

"Chris Holiday." He shook the meaty hand, but noted the grip wasn't unfriendly.

"Ah, you took the new house off Pine Street."

"That's the one." He beamed to cover his dismay at the town sheriff knowing exactly where he lived.

"Welcome to Blitzen."

"Thank you." Drex picked up a head of lettuce.

"If you're looking to meet some townsfolk, there is a Christmas dance on the 20th and a big food drive with the parade on December 21st."

"Thank you, Sheriff. I'll keep those in mind."

HOLLY DROVE downtown and parked on Main Street near the bistro.

"Isn't it gorgeous?" she asked Figgy, who hovered in the passenger seat beside her. Now that he was here, she had someone with whom to enjoy the decorations.

"A lovely display of Christmas cheer / A harbinger of fortune this coming year."

Snow topped the eaves and lined the sidewalks. Each street lantern bore a giant, shimmering golden snowflake. During the day, the tinsel sparkled, and at night, the lights glowed. Green wreaths with vibrant red poinsettias and berries adorned storefront doors near windows framed in Christmas lights.

Holly zipped up her winter coat, pulled on her gloves, and tugged her hat over her head. "Are you coming or staying?"

"I'll watch you from afar / I'll stay here in the car. If you need me, say the word / I'll fly to you like a bird."

Based on their past encounters, she knew Figgy often kept his distance when she entered crowds. Since she was the only person who could see and hear him and she didn't want to be the strange woman talking to herself, she was content to update him on events later. Somehow though, he was also able to watch her without her seeing him.

She hopped out of the car and walked to the bistro where she held the door open for Mrs. Whitaker.

"Holly, how are you?"

"I'm great. Are you planning Christmas with Patrick and Penelope?"

"Oh, yes. A big get together since Manny is the first grandchild in the family."

Patrick and Penelope were a couple Holly and Figgy had paired two years ago. She worked at the bank, and he was a veterinarian. Together, they had three dogs and child number one.

"How about you, Holly?"

Although she suspected Mrs. Whitaker was asking about family, she opted to skirt the question. "I'll be at the Christmas dance. Hope to see you there."

As the women exchanged Merry Christmas's, they went different directions inside the bistro.

Warm air engulfed Holly as she walked toward the counter. She wasn't hungry, so she ordered tea and took a seat. Glancing around the shop, she saw mostly townspeople she knew—the retired Jones brothers who spent their afternoon playing chess at the rec center, the town counselor, Candy Ackers, and Sheriff Joe Carpenter who was growing his beard out again to play Santa at the parade. Others were tourists not fulfilling the demographic of the man she sought to have a 'chance' encounter with—Chris Holiday.

She realized her poor planning as she scanned the room a second time—she didn't know what this mystery man looked like, and Figgy wasn't close by to point him out.

She pulled out her phone and elected to do a search.

Ugh. There were too many Chris Holidays, and although she knew he was a consultant, she didn't know his company's name. She might have to summon Figgy to point him out to her.

All thoughts of the newcomer vanished when Holly caught sight of the profile of a handsome man at the check-out counter. He had brown hair and dark brown eyes. His oval face held a strong jaw with trim facial hair and a straight nose.

"Drex?" she said tentatively, but the slight tensing of his shoulders told her that her instincts were spot on. She stood and gave a friendly smile. "Drex Alister?"

He hesitated, as if debating if he would acknowledge her. When he lifted his head in her direction, she smiled.

He greeted her smile with a tentative quirk of his lips —not unfriendly but carrying a hint of irritation to suggest she'd interrupted or intruded, perhaps his lunch break. He was dressed in jeans, a grey sweater, and a faux fur-lined black coat.

"Do I know you?" he asked.

She walked closer, suddenly embarrassed by her

outburst. Of course, he wouldn't remember her. She had been a freshman crushing on a senior who barely knew she existed.

Drex stared at the vibrant blonde woman approaching him. Blue jeans hugged slender legs, and a candy cane T-shirt gave her a festive look.

She gave a more tentative smile as she turned her paper cup in her hands. "Not really. We went to the same high school."

High school? Of all things—first the sheriff and now someone from high school identified him in remote Maryland?

"James Madison High?" She looked like she really wanted him to remember her, but he didn't.

High school had been three different schools and three different foster homes. He didn't remember much of anyone from his nine months of senior year in Brooklyn.

He did, however, recognize this woman from the pictures he'd seen of her realtor business. He glanced around the room, noting that the two of them were drawing the attention of patrons.

She waved a hand. "You don't remember, it's okay. Never mind. I'm sorry I bothered you." A flush creeping up from her neck threatened to reach and merge with a pair of reddening cheeks.

He'd rather see her beaming smile on that lovely face framed in blonde curls than the way she retreated into a shell of insecurity.

"Not a bother at all," he said. "High school was a long time ago. Maybe you can jog my memory."

When her smile returned in full force, the bistro became suddenly warm and cramped.

"Do you want to walk and talk?" He gestured toward the door.

"I always prefer walking to sitting," she replied in a chipper voice. She set down her drink long enough to zip her coat and put on her gloves and hat.

Drex found himself smiling; apparently, hers was contagious. He opened the door and was grateful for the blast of cold air that struck him. Surely, he'd been warm because she'd identified him and not because she was an attractive woman close to his age. He had no time for a relationship, and certainly no intention of endangering someone by proximity.

"James Madison High. You came in new and no one knew you," she said.

Story of my life, he thought.

She continued, "You didn't have a of Brooklyn accent. You kind of had this aloof vibe like you were too cool for school."

Drex laughed, startling Holly.

"I don't know about cool. I mostly wanted to keep my head down and graduate."

They walked side by side down the sidewalk lined with storefronts.

"How did you end up in this town?" Drex asked.

"Fresh start three years ago. I visited this place once with my family, and the beauty of it stuck with me."

A fresh start? He could relate to that, but he wondered

what had been important for Holly to leave behind? He shook off the thought. No attachments. He might not be here long enough to form anything meaningful.

"Blizten is a magnificent little town," he agreed. Main Street was picture perfect. Despite his many drops and exchanges in big cities and the blissful anonymity a metropolis offered, small shops in a central cozy town captured his affection.

"How did *you* end up here?" she asked.

"Fresh start."

"What do you do?" she asked.

"Consulting. And you are in real estate."

"How'd you know?"

"Your poster is on the billboard on the drive into town. Holly Sanders."

"Ah, right."

He would have to also come clean about his alter ego. In a small town like this, she was bound to run into people who referred to him as Chris Holiday—such as Sheriff Carpenter. If he didn't get in front of the lie, it would only arouse suspicion.

"As the superstar town relator, perhaps you can give me the tour," he suggested. Who better than to give him the inside scoop on everything he needed to know?

That thousand-watt smile of hers sent a zing through him which he instantly squelched.

No attachments.

CHAPTER 4

*D*rex walked arm and arm with Holly down the center of town.

"Let's start with main street," she began. "For shops, there Mila's Boutique, Charity's Charm, Akar's Jewelers, Toy World, Tony's Wine Bar, Blitzen Antiques, and more." She continued to rattle of places and the names of owners.

"There are thirty-eight buildings on the National Historic Register. Upcoming events include Classical Christmas, which is a dinner and candlelight concert at the Montgomery Museum sponsored by the Blitzen Heritage Foundation. Every second Friday is live music and sidewalk sales downtown—when it's not freezing. Oh," she pointed to two white horses and a carriage, "and carriage rides. Crime is forty percent lower than the US average. We are only fifteen miles from the Ocean City boardwalk."

"You're a regular encyclopedia." With a memory like

that, maybe *she* should have been a spy. He suspected she'd committed all of this to memory for her job in real estate.

"Let's go inside the bakery." She steered him across the street. "Janet and her daughter Regina are phenomenal bakers. Chocolate eclairs to die for. One taste and you'll want to be best friends—or more. She's single." At her last statement, she gave him a sheepish grin.

When he didn't follow her inside, she let the door close and returned to his side. "Everything okay?"

"Look, Holly—" If he went inside, she would introduce him as Drex. But he wanted to spread the name Chris Holiday as much as possible. There would still be damage control from her calling him Drex at the bistro, but the more people who came to know him as Chris, the better.

"I'm sorry." She grimaced. "I shouldn't have made the *single* comment. It's just that I have this compulsion to match-make during the holiday season. I noticed you don't have a ring and... and I over-stepped."

She took a step as if to walk away from the bakery, and her footing gave way ever so slightly. The motion was too minuscule to even call it a slip. Still, he linked his arm through hers, not willing to risk her repeating the motion and slipping. He kept his bistro box lunch in the other.

Drex led her down the sidewalk. "Don't fret about it. But I definitely don't require your matching-making services. I have no problem being single for the holidays. I have been all my life." He'd spent time with women in a romantic capacity, but nothing long enough to be called a relationship. Part of him hoped parading Holly on his arm down Main Street would deter all other women from approaching him.

"That's depressing," she said.

He chuckled. "The reason I appeared as the new kid in high school and seemed aloof was because I was in and out of foster homes. Christmas was usually an outside looking in event. Eventually, I realized I didn't really need holidays."

He wasn't sure why he opened up to Holly—perhaps because she'd somehow remembered him after all these years. He'd never considered himself worth remembering.

"Everybody needs holidays."

"What about you?" he asked.

"I love the holidays."

"So, do you stay in Blitzen or visit home for Christmas?" He wondered if home was back in Brooklyn or if she'd been a transplant too.

She chucked her empty cup in a trash can. "I am home."

He ran a tongue along his teeth. He suspected the terse reply, masked with forced cheer, was related to the fresh start she'd mentioned. A story lurked behind that "fresh start," but he didn't need to know it.

"Are you celebrating with someone?" But he knew the answer.

She was obviously not engaged or married—she'd been alone at the bistro, she hadn't pulled away when he'd linked arms, and she wasn't worried about public opinion of being seen arm-in-arm with a man.

"I celebrate by bringing people together."

"Whoa. Would you look at that?" Drex stopped and gaped at a bookstore. The exterior was navy with gold trim. Twinkling lights framed the large windows. The inside display was a glowing scene of miniature people reading books in a winter wonderland of wreaths, Christmas trees, and snow.

Before he knew what he was doing, he pulled out the postcard.

Holly leaned toward him. "It's a similar style, isn't it? Where did you get that photograph from?"

When he entered the store, she followed.

"This one is just a dream." He waved the postcard in the air before tucking it back in his pocket. "This one is real." His gaze roamed around the shop. The smell of books filled his nostrils—paperback and hardback, new and vintage. A faint scent of cinnamon also hung in the air. "I've dreamed of owning a bookstore like this on a street like this. But I want a bigger room for a coffee bar, some tables, and a couch." He clamped his mouth shut and glanced at Holly. He'd never shared his bookstore dream with anyone—not even Chester.

Holly's eyes sparkled while she looked around as though visualizing the dream with him.

Feeling oddly exposed, he exited the shop. "Just a dream."

As if sensing his discomfort, she looped her arm back through his. "It's a beautiful dream. Everyone has to have dreams. And maybe someone to share them with."

He suppressed an admiring chuckle at her innuendo. As a spy, he knew how to plant the seeds of ideas to reap later. She was good, but he wouldn't let his appreciation of her talent show; he didn't want to encourage her. They reached the end of the lane, and he took her toward Pine Street.

"I would appreciate if you didn't add me to your match-making efforts," he reiterated.

"Are you sure? I know several eligible women your age. Maybe you just need a little more time to settle." Her voice held a teasing tone.

Settle.

That was as fanciful a notion as becoming a bookstore owner.

HOLLY'S MIND had raced with the prospect of connecting Drex with one of the eligible women in Blitzen, but he'd effectively squashed those plans. No problem. She had other people to skillfully weave together. She could circle back around to him later.

Perhaps Drex needed a different type of Christmas miracle. She wondered if she could help him achieve his bookstore dream. She realized they'd walked several blocks from Main Street as she let her scheming plan marinate.

He stopped in front of a four-bedroom house with white siding and blue window trims. She knew this house.

"This is my new house," Drex announced.

She frowned. "No, I sold this to someone else."

"Yes. You sold it to my *nom de plume*—Chris Holiday."

"Why do you have a pseudonym? I thought you did consulting?" Even as she said the word, she realized she didn't know what that meant exactly. She'd never asked him to elaborate on his career.

He pulled his arm away, turned, and faced her. "Like you, I needed a fresh start."

His gaze met hers in something close to a dare. She started to open her mouth to ask what he meant, but thought better of it. Asking him why he needed a fresh start would pave the way to him asking her, and she didn't need to rehash the misery.

"Do you like the house?" she asked.

"It's perfect."

"Seems big for one person."

"I like my space."

"I guess so after growing up in foster care."

He seemed to consider her analysis and accept it. "Perhaps you're right."

"What about the furniture? Was it to your liking?" She'd been happy to sell the house, but had also coveted it for some time. It was walking distance to Main Street, and she'd dreamed of having a location like this near town. The home was also new and not the fixer-upper in which she'd invested.

"You did great," he said.

His sincere compliment sent a wave of heat through her. *Oh.* She was standing very close to a single man whose house she intimately knew—bedroom sizes, furniture, bathroom layouts, and kitchen appliances. She swallowed and took a step back from him.

Drex looked puzzled by her distancing. "I appreciate everything you did, and I'm sorry for having to work with you remotely for the purchase."

"No problem. Do I call you Chris or Drex?" she asked.

"I like Drex so much better, but if you could use Chris in public, I would appreciate it."

She threaded her gloved fingers together. In public.

When would they be in private? Was he assuming there would be a private moment? They stood on the sidewalk, just the two of them, in a winter wonderland. Was this one of those private moments, or was this public?

When had the December air become so thick?

She eased another step back from him. "Chris. Yes. Got it."

"And, I got your gift basket."

"Oh, good."

"A thoughtful touch," he added. "Can I walk you back into town?"

"You're home, and I have errands to run." She continued to walk backward.

"Are you okay? I feel like I've made you uncomfortable with the name thing."

She shook her head. "No, no. The name is fine." She wrapped knuckles against her head as she continued to back away. "I've got it locked in my vault of a memory."

He chuckled. "Then I know my secret is safe with you."

HOLLY WALKED BACK toward her car in a daze. Chris Holiday was none other Drex Alister whom she'd briefly crushed on in high school. What were the odds? Now, Figgy's statement about meeting him *again* made sense.

She rubbed her inner elbow where her arm had been linked with Drex's. The closeness had been unexpected, especially as they were essentially strangers. He'd rejoined arms after she'd had a slight misstep on an icy patch. She hadn't been close to falling, and the timing wasn't as though he was catching her. He'd been a gentleman, without implying he thought she couldn't walk on her own. He offered a safety net without judgment and seemed genuinely pleased when she'd appreciated his offer.

"You're such a klutz, Holly." The voice from her past rang in her ears.

Unlike the man she'd left behind, her exchange with Drex hadn't felt the least bit derogatory.

She straightened and brushed strands of hair off her cheek. She needed to focus on the initial task. Drex Alister was Chris Holiday, and the man was desperately in need of some Christmas cheer. True, he believed he didn't want to meet someone this holiday, but everyone says such nonsense when faced with the potential of someone matchmaking. What Drex didn't understand was that she and Figgy worked covertly, and their efforts would feel nothing as awkward as a blind date.

She weighed her options. Regina at the bakery, Linda the dentist, or Hope, the interior decorator.

When she reached her car, she unlocked the door and sat in the driver's seat. Figgy appeared beside her.

"Well, I met Chris Holiday." Her gaze slid to the ghost and then back to the wheel as she started the car.

"I saw the exchange entirely / and you're not thinking clearly," Figgy said.

"Of course I am. We're going to make this holiday great. You were watching us? Did you hear the part about the bookstore? The other day at the bistro, I heard Pickens talking about maybe selling the place. I can look into that more. The adjacent shop is for sale. If Drex bought both, he could knock out the wall and have his bookstore with his coffee shop combined. But that might be a little too much space. Well, I suppose you just fill the space with more bookshelves."

"Drex might be your toughest case / take care, and you must make haste."

Holly drove them back to her place. "I specialize in haste. Quality and speed."

"Holly, slow down and stop being a spaz. You get so sloppy sometimes."

She shook off the criticizing voice in her head.

"So, what is your holiday mojo telling you?" she asked Figgy as she forced a smile. She listed off the names of prospective women for Drex.

The elf was silent a moment before narrowing his eyes at her in a calculating look. "To succeed in our endeavor / two he must meet / But that Drex is clever / We'll need to be discreet."

"Discreet and hasty? I am up for a challenge." She pulled into her driveway and shot a disparaging look at her house.

She was up for a challenge, was she? She had certainly given herself a challenge when she bought this house. On the bright side, she had all afternoon to sand the floors and conspire with Figgy.

Zielinski stopped his online day trading to take a phone call.

"It's Donna."

"Has there been a development?" Zielinski asked the

CIA officer. He debated if he should prophylactically take an antacid anytime she called, and he opened his drawer just in case.

"Yeah. We got a flag on Drex Alister. Sheriff in a town in Maryland was looking up the name in a few databases."

Zielinski bit back the urge to swear as he tightened his left hand into a ball. Three weeks had passed, and he'd had no news of Drex's whereabouts. He'd hoped that meant the ex-spy had slunk into a hidey-hole for good, but successfully disappearing in the electronic era wasn't easy.

"That's great news." He forced the words out of his mouth, glad Donna couldn't see his expression. "I hope you catch him. He tarnished my company's good name. What did the sheriff say?" He opened the bottle and tossed two chalky tablets into his mouth.

"We didn't want to alarm him that the CIA would be visiting his little town of Blitzen. Hopefully, we can quietly send our man in and deal with Drex without alerting any local authorities."

"Reasonable plan. Thanks for keeping me in the loop. Who are you sending, if I may ask?"

"Spinner."

A smile spread across Zielinski's lips. Stan Spinner. Excellent. The CIA was sending a known assassin. The man didn't miss and had a reputation for being quick and clean. Drex would never know what hit him.

Donna hung up the phone, and Zielinski stared at it with dubious delight. He would be relieved when the CIA dealt with Drex, and he wouldn't have to continue to look over his shoulder. Ever since the Prague debacle, he'd felt like his reflux was slowly transforming into an erosive ulcer as acid burned through the lining.

He looked at the date on his computer. December 15th. His problem would be handled in the next few days and would feel like an early Christmas present.

*P*uzzling on Holly's strange behavior, Drex let himself into his house. He'd enjoyed walking with her and immersing in her bubbly personality. She had beautiful hair and true-blue eyes—earnest, honest blue. He'd never met a woman like her—all genuine warmth and smiles. But some of that behavior was a brave front—for what, he wasn't sure.

None of his business.

After shrugging off his coat, he peeled off his black tactical shooting gloves. He'd worn them for warmth, but they were also the only gloves he ever wore. The thin material meant he could fit his hand into the trigger hole to fire a gun, and yet they still kept his fingers warm.

He washed his hands before taking his bistro sandwich to the table and sitting down. As he ate, he perused his secure email on his laptop. Nothing from any of his contacts. He'd done favors over the years for defectors and other spies, but now that he was burned, he might never be able to cash in on those. Yet, he would check messages regularly in the event someone felt obligated to warn him if his new identity was compromised or had the urge to pass on any information about Ludvik's death that might exonerate Drex. But he couldn't count on that definitely happening.

He used his burner phone and called Chester.

"You're supposed to be enjoying your new home," Chester said in lieu of a "hello."

"Hard to enjoy anything when you feel like there's a target on your back," he said.

"Try. To. Relax," she said.

"You haven't heard anything?"

"Nobody knows where you are."

Was she saying that based on intuition or just the absence of knowledge? And if she was out of the business like he was, what connections did she still have?

"Let's hope I can keep it that way. So far, local law enforcement has introduced himself, and I was recognized by someone from my high school." He had registered his gun to carry it concealed, which could raise alarms if law enforcement did an inquiry on his new identity. If Sheriff Carpenter discovered the licensed weapon, he might be prompted to dig into Chris Holiday's past. When he didn't find much, he might dive deeper for answers and wouldn't like what he would find.

"A high school buddy?" Chester asked.

"I didn't have high school *buddies*. This is a woman. The local town realtor."

"Were you a heart-breaker in high school?"

He scowled into the phone. "Impossible. I didn't date anyone in high school. I was a loner—no friends, no girls."

Chester grunted. "Seems not much has changed. This woman remembered you—fifteen years later. You must have made some kind of impression. Maybe it's a sign you need to stop being a loner."

He logged into his laptop and did a quick search of his alma mater. "A relationship in the midst of my situation would be irresponsible. Someone could get hurt. Besides, I think she's the type of person who remembers everybody—some type of cataloging brain, which is why she's successful in sales." He went back fifteen years and found evidence of Holly Sanders having attended his high school. She was who she claimed to be and had remembered him accurately.

"Uh-huh," Chester said.

He roughly closed his laptop. "Look, I didn't call to talk about relationships." What had gotten into Chester, anyway? "Can you just keep an ear to the ground so you can give me a heads up if you hear about trouble coming my way?"

"Always."

"Thanks, Chester. And I'm sorry for being the cause of your early retirement."

If she hadn't been protecting him, she might have been able to stay under Zielinski. Unless Zielinski was behind Prague, as Drex suspected, in which case he'd done Chester a favor and kept her from being Zielinski's next pawn.

"It was time," she said simply.

When he hung up the phone, he fidgeted with his

watch and withdrew the small USB hidden within it. He still had Ludvik's information, though the file he'd downloaded to his phone was encrypted. Drex had transferred the information onto a USB, but he didn't have access to the type of software needed to unlock it. Plus, he already knew from Ludvik that this was only partial information, and he didn't know who now possessed the other piece.

He wanted to finish the job and turn what he had over to the US government, but he wasn't sure who he could trust. With his burned status, friends might now be enemies, and who knew what lies Zielinski might be spreading.

He twirled the USB in his fingers, resigned to waiting. Most of spy work was patience and building relationships. He would have to bide his time and wait for an opening. If Chester learned anything, she'd let him know.

Unlike the movies, he didn't muscle his way into saving the day. And there was certainly no dashing through the snow or chasing down leads with the clock ticking—well, except for the bomb in Amsterdam, but that had been an isolated incident.

HOLLY SAT in the bistro across from Linda, whom she'd convinced to join her on a lunch date. Three days had passed since running into Drex at this very place. So much for haste. But Holly had gotten bogged down in work, and this was the next best "chance" encounter she and Figgy had concocted.

"Do you have Christmas plans?" Holly asked Linda.

"I'll close up shop on the twenty-third and drive to upstate New York to see my brother." Linda had short chestnut hair and the perfectly white teeth people expected of their dentist.

Holly nodded, a little disappointed Linda hadn't said she'd be here alone for Christmas—that would have been a better opening for discussing Drex—er—Chris.

"How about you?" Linda asked.

"Here alone." Holly chewed her lip. "How about the Christmas dance? Are you going? Do you have a date?"

Linda swallowed a bite of her Philly cheesesteak sandwich. Holly couldn't help but think she'd need extra mouth mints before going back to work after consuming those onions. With those vibrant teeth, she probably brushed after every meal.

"No date. Who has time for that?" Linda sipped her diet Coke.

"You can make time."

"I date—you should see my collection of romance novels."

"That's not dating. Dating is companionship." Holly toyed with the straw in her drink.

"I happen to think I don't need a man to complete me."

"Everybody needs companionship. And it can be for fulfillment, not because of some notion that you're incomplete."

"So, how come I don't see you chasing a man?" Linda fired back at her with a playfully accusing tone.

"Okay. First of all, *chasing a man* is not dating. It's just wrong that you associate the two that way. Secondly, it's taken three years to build my self-esteem back after the last man. Thirdly, I'm in the contempla-tive stage."

Linda blinked at her. "There are detailed stages?"

"Of course! Just like buying a house—or any change in life. Precontemplation, contemplation, preparation, and action." She ticked them off one finger at a time.

"Then I guess I'm in contemplation, too."

The doorbell jingled as Drex entered the bistro. Giddy excitement bubbled through Holly. Figgy had predicted Drex would come here for lunch, and now Holly's plan was falling into place.

When he saw her, they exchanged waves before he stood in line to place his order.

Linda glanced over her shoulder. "Oh. Are you sure you're not in the action stage?"

Holly gave a nervous chuckle. She couldn't tell Linda she was immersed in the action stage of helping other people. "He's a friend. But I'll see if he can join us." Her plan was to have Drex join them for lunch and then Holly would spontaneously remember she needed to meet with a client about a house.

With wrapped sandwich in hand, Drex approached their table. Holly had suspected, gentleman that he was, that he would come say hello even though he'd gotten his food to go and would have left otherwise.

"Hi! How's your day?" she asked.

"Good. Thanks. I got your message about the book-store. I'm going to stop by there tomorrow."

She turned toward Linda. "This is Linda Gilbert. She's a dentist here in town."

"Chris Holiday. Nice to meet you."

His smile sent warmth through Holly. Maybe this would work.

Linda's pager buzzed. "Oh. That's me. I need to go." She scrambled to wrap her sandwich in the paper around it and stuffed it in her oversized purse.

Holly stood as she stood. "You have to go?"

"Duty calls."

"You wear a pager?" Drex mused.

"Dentists, doctors, and drug dealers. We're the last group clinging to old technology. But it works."

Shocked at the turn of events, Holly watched Linda leave the bakery. Figgy had been wrong about the timing of events here. Figgy was never wrong.

"Do you want some company?" Drex asked.

She tried to compose herself. "Um. Yes. That would be great."

He took a seat and unwrapped his Italian sub.

Holly sat back down, recovering her composure. "Linda is a fantastic person. She normally doesn't vanish like that. Must have been an oral emergency. She's a career woman, but has weekends off. She has a boat in Ocean City and goes sailing during the summer."

Drex had lifted his sandwich toward his mouth, where it hovered as he listened to her.

Unbitten, he set his sandwich back down. "You're not very subtle about your ongoing attempts at match-making."

She lifted one shoulder and didn't attempt to conceal the guilty look she knew she wore. "I'm not a subtle person."

He chuckled. "I'm still not interested."

She stuck out her bottom lip in a pout as she contemplated her next move. She didn't want to pursue a topic that would detract from his enjoyment of his lunch break.

"Okay." She snatched a pen out of her purse and unfolded a clean paper napkin. "Let's talk about that bookstore."

He gave her an adorable grin and took a bite of his sub. She wondered if she could still soften him up to the idea of spending Christmas with a special someone.

She drew as she spoke. "This rectangle is the bookstore. The rows of shelves are tight together. If you expanded it to include the unoccupied shop next door, you'd get this." She extended the rectangle to a larger square. "The cafe could go here with seating here and little tables beside them for drinks. Hope—she's an interior decorator—could probably suggest some unique mood lighting for the sitting area." She cleared her throat and looked up, worried she'd gotten carried away. "Depending on your budget."

The dreamy look in his eyes as he stared at her sketch suggested he could picture her description. "It's brilliant. The lights should be golden and strung low from the ceiling. The sitting area should be earthen tones for warm comfort."

"You've thought about this."

"I've been in a lot of bookstores. But, yes, I'll also have to look into my budget."

They continued the conversation about bookstores and places Drex had traveled as they ate their sandwiches.

When they finished, Drex stood. "Thanks for the

company. I enjoyed lunch with you." He folded the napkin with the floor plan and put it in his pocket.

"Yes, me too." She pulled on her coat, hat, and gloves.

"Oh. I did want to ask you if I can get my other spare key back from you." He shrugged into his coat.

"Absolutely. I have other work this afternoon. I can come tomorrow, bring it to your place."

"Sounds good."

DREX LEFT the bistro and crossed the street. He looked back to see Holly getting into her car.

When he looked up and noticed he was in front of the bakery, he thought he'd try those eclairs Holly had raved about, while also doing a little reconnaissance. He needed to know more about the town and more about its gregarious relator. How much of a security threat to him did Holly pose?

When he pulled open the door, the bells on a festive wreath jingled. It seemed every shop in this town had jingle bells. The bakery smelled like cinnamon, vanilla, and chocolate.

A woman in her mid-fifties stood behind the counter drying her hands. "Can I help you?" Her voice was cheerful.

"Yes. I'd like a chocolate eclair." He withdrew his wallet.

"Just one? It's half-off the second." She pointed to the prices on a large chalkboard on the back wall.

"Twist my arm. I'll take two."

"Also, we're taking orders now for Christmas cakes

and pies. We'll reach capacity soon, so you'll want to place your order now."

"I won't need any of those, thanks."

"Going back home for the holidays?"

"I am home. I moved into the new house on Pine Street. Chris Holiday."

Her smile brightened. "Oh. Holly mentioned a newcomer." She turned her head. "Regina, order up front!" she called toward the back room.

A woman emerged from the back wearing an apron and her raven dark hair pulled back. She had her mother's oval face and round nose.

"I'm Janet, and this is my daughter, Regina. Regina, Chris just moved to town."

When the baker smiled at her daughter, a mischievous glint in her eye told Drex that Holly wasn't the only person who might threaten to try to set him up in a relationship.

"Nice to meet you. I moved in on Pine Street, bought it from Holly. She recommended this bakery."

Janet busied herself boxing two eclairs.

"I'll be sure to thank her," Regina said, subtly fluttering long eyelashes.

"Have you been friends long?" he asked.

"Since she moved here about three years ago."

"She's a fantastic relator—even picked out furniture for me. Is she seeing anyone?"

The corners of Regina's mouth fell slightly.

Drex knew she would infer that he was romantically interested in Holly. Although he wasn't, feigning interest in her to others would ward off unwanted advances. Yes, he could take this angle—and since Holly had retreated from him awkwardly the first day they'd met and tried to set him up with the town dentist, she clearly wasn't interested in a relationship. As such, he wasn't in danger of hurting her feelings. And she might never know.

"No." Regina shook her head. "I haven't seen Holly with anyone, and if she was dating someone, this place is one of the first places she'd bring a man."

He puzzled on that a moment since the bakery had been the first place Holly had tried to take him.

Janet rang up his order, and he paid in cash.

"Do you think I'm her type?" He gave a winning smile as he walked toward the door.

"I honestly don't know," Regina said. "I don't think she's dated anyone since moving here."

"Oh." Drex faltered. He'd intended on slipping out the door and congratulating himself on achieving his deception, but genuine concern stopped him in his tracks. "Why is that?"

This was a small town, but Holly must have some dating options.

Regina's expression softened at the concern in his voice. She opened her mouth, but her mother shooed her away.

"Those cakes aren't going to cook themselves."

Regina cast an apologetic look toward Drex as she returned to the back room. Janet busied herself straightening pastries.

He guessed that concluded the conversation. "Nice meeting you. Thanks for the eclairs."

As he exited the bakery, the cold bit in to his cheeks

and ears. He scanned the premises, the hair on his neck raising slightly. But he didn't see anyone watching him. He saw some familiar and some unfamiliar faces as people moved along Main Street and in and out of stores. Townspeople and tourists traveling at different paces, but all preparing for the holiday.

But some had a few shifty behaviors he was learning more about each time he ventured into town. The bank president flirted a bit too much with the diner waitress twenty years younger than him. The grocery store stock boy played with a butane lighter on his breaks. Drex didn't know how to walk through life without observing everything and everyone around him.

Walking home, he considered this new insight into Holly. She'd claimed she'd moved here for a fresh start, and he'd wondered if she'd run away from some part of her past. Now, he contemplated if she'd never made that fresh start and was still living under the shadow of her past.

Nope. Not going there. He absolutely did not want to delve into Holly's past or present.

No attachments.

He walked home and dropped the eclairs on the counter, but hadn't satisfied his urge for information gathering. He got in his car and explored the outer limits of the town, including a drive by Holly's real-estate office and her home.

She lived in an older home in need of a paint job. When he glimpsed the back porch and noticed crooked and missing planks, he wondered about the safety of the place. Was she struggling to make ends meet or did she want the challenge of a fixer-upper?

Why did he want to know?

He pictured her leaning over the napkin, putting thought and energy into his bookstore idea—investing time *in him*. Her interest in others' well-being fascinated him, and he wanted to learn what made her tick.

He snuffed the idea as he drove home.

No attachments.

CHAPTER 6

*H*olly stopped at the bakery to pick up eclairs. She had texted Drex to let him know she would deliver the requested spare key to him. She decided to concurrently bring some of Regina's cooking to him. Perhaps once he tasted the divinity of her dessert, he would be receptive to becoming acquainted with her when the opportunity presented itself.

"Morning, Regina. Two eclairs please."

"Holly, good to see you. How is the house coming along?"

She tugged off one of her gloves and held up her hands for Regina to see the blisters and Band-Aids. "It might be the death of me."

"Death by a thousand cuts?"

"That, or the roof will cave in." *Or the back porch,* she thought. But she never ventured out onto the hazard since the first time she felt the instability beneath her feet.

"You should hire Winston to help with that."

"I might." But if she paid for every repair the house needed, she'd go broke.

Holly decided to change the subject. "So, there's a new guy in town." She wiggled her eyebrows and leaned closer as she lowered her voice to a conspiratorial whisper. "Cute and single."

"Chris Holiday. We met." Regina rung up her order.

"You did?" Holly straightened, then brightened. "You did," she repeated. Maybe they'd already struck a chord together.

"I did. And boy, is he interested in you."

"Me?" Holly fumbled with her credit card before inserting it into the reader.

"Yeah. Asked if you were seeing anyone."

"Oh."

This wasn't going according to plan. Drex was supposed to be interested in Regina. Maybe he was just curious. Maybe he hadn't tasted whatever he'd ordered yet and therefore couldn't yet fall for Regina's special superpower—delicious sweets.

And why would he ask Regina about her? She hadn't flirted with him, and she'd been very clear that the matchmaking was with someone else. Had she sent him mixed signals?

"Holly?"

She jumped. "Yes?"

Regina looked down at the electronic reader. "You can take your card out."

"Oh, right." Holly pulled it out, put it in her purse, and took the packaged eclairs. She thanked Regina and tugged her glove back on before she left.

She started walking toward Drex's house. "Figgy?"

He appeared beside her, the bell on his hat jingling.

"Did you hear that? Drex was asking about me. What should I do?"

"You haven't a clue?"

"No. That's why I'm asking you. Ugh. Now, I'm rhyming."

"If sparks aren't flying / those plans are dying."

"Okay. Not Regina. How about Linda? I'm trying to get her to go to the Christmas dance. She always comes. Can I hook them up them there?"

"Perhaps, but you'll need to prepare."

She reached Drex's house and stepped onto his porch. "What does that mean? Prepare what?"

But Figgy vanished as Drex swung his door open.

Wow. She hadn't even knocked yet. Had he installed some type of door sensor?

"Holly, thanks for coming."

"Your spare key." She held it up. "And eclairs."

"Thank you. Although, I did take your advice and try them already."

As he took the bag, she made an obvious show of trying to peer around him at the inside of his house. "Yes, Regina told me you two met." She grinned.

Before he could open his mouth—probably in some form of objection to her trying to match him—she said, "Your house is still bare. You haven't unpacked yet?"

He arched an eyebrow as if to convey his displeasure at her intrusiveness.

She shivered and bounced on the balls of her toes.

He deflated slightly as he stepped aside and gestured

to his foyer. "Would you like to come inside?" His tone suggested he'd asked out of politeness but didn't actually want company.

Holly's smile widened. Oh, he was *not* into her. Regina must have misread their interaction at her bakery.

She stepped inside the glorious warmth with renewed determination at her match-making scheme. After slipping off her boots, she walked around the living room and into the kitchen where Drex began putting each eclair on a plate.

She tugged off her knit hat and patted her hair down. "You haven't done anything yet. No decorations. No furniture except the stuff I bought you."

He poured two glasses of water before sliding a glass and an eclair over to her. "What's the rush?"

"No rush." She picked at the edge of the pastry as she leaned on the counter. "But most people have a few personal effects they put out right away. You don't even have boxes lining the walls to unpack."

He stood on the opposite side of the jutting countertop and took a bite of eclair as he stared at her.

"Oh. Have they not delivered your belongings?" She wondered if the snow had delayed his shipment.

He swallowed a gulp of water. "What you see is what you get. A fresh start." The same challenge lit his eyes as the other day—as if she was supposed to let the topic of conversation die there and she wouldn't like the repercussions of digging.

She understood the discussion would be tit for tat—she'd have to be willing to explain her fresh start if he was going to share his. Standing in his kitchen, eating his dessert, and watching him move in those blue jeans made diving into that conversation easier than she'd expected.

"I didn't bring much with me when I made my fresh start," she said.

He crossed his arms, but his voice was deep and gentle. "Why is that?"

"I ran away on my wedding day."

He blinked as his mouth opened in surprise. "Ran away?"

She continued to pick at the dessert without taking another bite. "It was a scene straight out of *Runaway Bride*. I started down the aisle and then bolted."

"Why did you run?"

"Fear." She slowly turned the plate on the counter. "The church had gorgeous stained-glass windows filtering golden light. White lilies and pink ribbon lined the aisle. It was a beautiful, sunny day. And I had a sudden cold, chest-squeezing realization that he was Mr. Wrong. Or at least the willingness to finally admit it."

"And you came here?"

"Haven't been home since." She turned her water glass in slow circles.

"So, you made a mistake. Or you avoided making one. Why would you not go home?"

"Everyone is fuming mad at me. They're upset with how I treated Harry."

"And you haven't dated since? Three years?"

She narrowed her eyes at him. "How do you know that?"

He shrugged. "Regina told me."

Regina. Right. Holly was here on a mission, which did

not include divulging her past, no matter how compassionate Drex's brown eyes turned.

She straightened. "Thank you for the eclair."

"You bought it."

"You shared. Anyway, I also wanted to make sure you knew about the Christmas dance on the twentieth. Lots of people will be there with live music and local beer."

"Are you asking me out on a date?"

She let out a nervous chuckle. "What? No. That was not my intention." Warmth crept from her neck up into her cheeks. She had been so masterful at her other matchmaking efforts over the years with Figgy. How was she repeatedly failing with Drex?

When he took a few steps closer, only a thin strip of counter separated them. "You were just being friendly?"

She tugged at her scarf, trying to loosen it so she could breathe. "Yes. I wanted to help you make Blitzen a home. Help you mingle and settle." Her eyes darted to the front door, calculating the shortest distance to escape.

"Are you this thoughtful to all your clients?" he asked.

"I like to think so." Perhaps she was friendlier with Drex because of the high school connection only she remembered. But truthfully, she knew nothing about this man aside from good manners and good looks.

"I should go." She swallowed.

"Holly." His voice sounded gentle. "If you want to leave, leave. I won't stop you. But please, don't be afraid of me. You look like I've frightened you, and I'd like to fix that. I'm sorry I accused you of asking me on a date."

Frightened? She wasn't afraid of Drex. Not like she had been of Harry.

"It's fine." She shrugged.

He remained so still and his face was so calm that she thought perhaps the safest place in the world was right at his side. Perhaps even directly in his arms.

On an exhale, she relaxed. "I'm not afraid of you. I have nervous energy sometimes."

"Your leg is bouncing again, Holly. Knock it off. Why haven't you started taking the anxiety pills your doctor prescribed for you?"

"Anyway," she cleared her throat, "I hope you'll consider going to the party." She walked past Drex and toward the door.

He reached it before her and opened it. "Will you be there?"

"Yes."

"Then so will I."

She bit back a smile. "Okay. See you there."

A block away, Holly's lightheadedness began to clear. Figgy appeared beside her as she walked toward her car parked outside the bakery.

She opened her door and climbed in the driver's seat. "That did *not* go as planned."

"He is going to the dance / that means there is a chance."

"Chance for what? He thought *I* was asking him on a date." She started the car and drove home.

"At the Christmas dance / you could give him a chance."

Her gaze snapped to Figgy and then back to the road. "You little devil. You knew Drex had already talked to

Regina. Did you know he would take my mention of the dance as a personal invitation?"

The elf ghost blinked rapidly but didn't answer.

She pulled into her drive and let the car idle. "Figgy," she implored, "My life is a mess. And I told you about Harry."

"Three years you've been away from home / three years and you're still alone. Drex needs you / you are the glue. Two fresh starts this Christmas season / his life saved—you'll be the reason."

Saved from what? she wondered. Loneliness, she presumed, judging by his house.

She killed the engine and sighed. "For once, I wish you didn't speak in riddles."

ZIELINSKI PARKED his car at the motel as he cursed the weather. His drive to Blitzen had been initially delayed followed by agonizingly slow travel through the snow. Thanks to the holiday season, the closest place for room and board was an hour's drive away from Drex Alister's hideout town.

Four days the CIA had known about Drex's location, and still Zielinski had received no word that his former employee had been eliminated. He didn't want to call Donna and ask—that would appear too desperate and tip them off that Zielinski considered Drex a loose end. He wanted to give the CIA the impression the loop was closed. He'd only received half his payment since the CIA had only retrieved partial information from the USB taken off Ludvik after his death. And Drex's reputation had been irrevocably damaged.

End of story.

Except Drex was still alive, and the ex-spy might try to clear his name.

Zielinski wanted this small-town operation to be a quick, easy in and out, but eliminating the burned spy would require a little planning, stealth, and creativity.

The problem was that he didn't know exactly where Drex was staying. He knew the town sheriff had looked up information on Drex, and the electronic search had triggered the CIA's Internet filter for the spy's name. But the ex-spy wasn't staying in this one-horse town under his real name. Zielinski had checked.

Since Zielinski didn't know his target's new identity or if he even still looked like the Drex that Zielinski had known, finding the former spy would require several days. And if he'd been savvy enough to hide under an alias not in the company's files, how had Drex slipped and let the sheriff know his real name? Was he getting sloppy in his early retirement, or was he laying a trap?

Fortunately, Blitzen wasn't a bustling metropolis. Zielinski only needed to stake out the few most likely places everyone in the town traveled—the diner, the gas station, and the grocery store.

After checking in and getting his room key, Zielinski pulled the suitcase out of his car. He'd only brought one weapon—his faithful Sig Sauer. There weren't any large buildings he could perch from for shooting a high-powered rifle, and he sure as heck wasn't about to sit in a tree in freezing weather waiting for his prey to pass his line of sight. Those days of his youth were long gone.

The situation was irksome, because the safest way to deal with a man like Drex Alister would be a five-hundred-yard kill-shot with a rifle—as had been the plan in Letná Park—and not under fifty yards with a handgun. A handgun meant Zielinski would need to get up close and personal with the ex-spy, who would have to be stationary long enough for him to fire. Yes, one more reason his attack would need to be calculated in order to succeed.

Zielinski carried his suitcase over the packed snow and ice as his footing threatened to slip several times. At last, he made it to the door, still standing, but the card took multiple swipes before it finally worked. Once inside the room, he slammed the door shut. Even inside the motel room, his breath condensed on the frigid air. He cranked on the room heater, which rattled absurdly loud while omitting fumes of burning dust.

The familiar dull, burning ache in his stomach radiated up to his center chest. These accommodations were beneath him. A few days of staying in these conditions and he'd be more than ready to shoot someone.

CHAPTER 7

rex threw Holly's partially nibbled eclair in the trash and cleaned his kitchen as he thought about his strange encounter with the woman. Another strange encounter. So why did he enjoy them so much?

She'd seemed genuinely sad at his lack of personal touch around the house. He'd never attached himself to places and objects, as these things weren't necessary for survival and didn't define who or what he was. As a relator, she seemed to think a house defined a person.

What did that say about her and her house in disrepair? She hadn't been treated well, and it seemed her emotions were in parallel disrepair to her home. She had a good heart, but busied herself thinking about other's wants and needs and not her own.

Who was Mr. Wrong? And why hadn't Holly moved on since him? What memories or events still haunted her? Why had she suddenly been afraid of Drex? Afraid of him or afraid of liking him?

Hmm. The woman who liked to match-make avoided romantic entanglements herself.

Did that make his plan to put on an appearance of interest in her a great idea or a terrible idea? If she was protecting her emotions and he accidentally lowered her walls, could he hurt her?

Would he be the next Mr. Wrong?

Because he did not want to hurt Holly, he needed a new plan. He saw two options. First, bow out of the dance while distancing himself from Holly. She would take the hint.

He barked out a laugh at that thought, startling himself. No, she wouldn't take the hint.

With a smile, he thought about how she'd nosed her way right into his house. And he clearly allowed her to plow through him—maybe even enjoyed it. Option two was to go to the dance and let Holly work her match-making magic. He could meet and politely dismiss whomever she attempted to set him up with. This could be weeks of exhaustive efforts on his part, but Holly would have the satisfaction of trying before realizing no one could manage his romantic life.

Yes, the long game was the way to play this. It wouldn't be too different from his spy work, which often took planning and patience.

HOLLY DONNED her red dress for the dance while swaying around the room and singing *Silver Bells*. She'd had a productive three days with selling a house and working on her own—including getting the flue working for her fireplace.

Throughout that time, she counted the hours to the dance. She tried to tell herself her excitement stemmed from the social event itself, but she also understood that when Drex agreed to attend because she would be there, something in the little protective bubble she'd constructed around herself had shifted.

She enjoyed his company and the way he was receptive to her energy and ideas. Was she moving from the contemplative stage to the planning stage after all? Was she ready for a relationship?

She wouldn't get ahead of herself. Tonight was only a dance.

Figgy appeared in her room.

She brushed her hair one last time. "Are you congratulating yourself? Your schemes to make me like Drex worked."

"When you have a friend so dear / you want to brighten her sphere."

She touched her hand to her heart. "You're incredibly sweet. You have brightened my sphere. And you're a dear friend, too. If you weren't a ghost, I'd hug you. But," she waggled a finger at him, "I'm not getting my hopes up. The man said he does not want a relationship. And, there will be other women at the dance."

"He has eyes only for you / you softened his heart, but there's more to do."

"I promise to be open to the idea of a relationship if Drex expresses interest. That's all I will agree to."

Figgy crossed his eyes and smiled, rosy round cheeks bulging.

THE CHRISTMAS PARTY was held at the rec center off main street. Holly parked her car and scurried into the building, hoping the salted walkway had been de-iced enough for her high heels. After checking her coat inside the front door, she entered the dance hall and marveled at the decorations. Golden snowflakes hung from the ceiling, and a twelve-foot-tall tree glowed brilliantly behind the band. Even though she'd been here every year for the last three years, it still held magic and wonder.

She lifted a glass of champagne off the serving tray and made the rounds to speak with everyone.

"Holly, how is the house coming?"

She grinned at Winston, a big, burly handyman who'd helped her with repairs on several houses she'd put on the market. "It's a work in progress."

"Call me, and we'll get her patched up."

"Thanks."

"Holly, good to see you," Janet said, looking lovely in a festive red and white dress. "Your pies will be ready for pickup the twenty-third."

"Excellent. Thank you." Holly had purchased pecan pies for all of her clients this year and had plans to pick them up and deliver all of them that day.

"Regina, you look fabulous," Holly said.

The baker smiled as she swished her green dress. "I

clean up all right. But I love the red on you." She leaned closer. "All decked out for Mr. Holiday?"

Holly could have argued that she'd planned to wear this dress before Drex even came to town, but she didn't think acting defensive would curb Regina's teasing.

"He's here, you know," Regina said. "And he wore a tux. An actual *tuxedo*."

Holly looked through the crowd, trying to spot him.

"Good luck." Regina elbowed her. "You're going to have to battle half the single women in Blitzen if you want that man."

Holly chuckled. Perhaps he would find someone, and her match-making this holiday would conclude with her own emotions unscathed. So why did she feel the slightest pang of jealously that Drex might dance with another woman tonight? Figgy was clearly turning her brain into pudding with all his talk of her finding love.

Sheriff Carpenter approached wearing brown slacks and a red and green plaid shirt. "Holly, pleasure to see you."

"Sheriff." She gave him a quick peck on his cheek just above his white beard. "You know Janet is here stag tonight." Holly winked.

He looked over his shoulder at the woman.

"You should ask her to dance, Joe," Holly encouraged.

He smiled. "I might do that. But I also came over to ask you a favor." He led her to a less crowded spot. "My elf is sick. I'm wondering if you could fill in tomorrow. I'm sorry for the short notice."

"The parade and the kids!" She thought about the consequences of no Santa's elf. Organizing children for visitation wouldn't happen, and chaos would ensue, making a magical occasion a nightmare for kids and parents. That was if Sheriff Carpenter wasn't forced to cancel the Santa visitation event entirely, which was volunteer run anyway.

"Can you help with both? The parade is just waving, but Santa's photo event is substantially more involved. I need you to keep the line of kids moving."

"I can help. Text me the details later."

"You're a life saver, Holly."

She caught a glimpse of Drex in his tuxedo talking to Regina. He looked stunning in black and white, holding a champagne flute.

The sheriff followed her gaze and then stepped into her line of sight. "You be careful with that one."

She frowned, looking up at him. "What do you mean?"

"I heard you call him Drex Alister in the bistro the other day, so I did a little background check on Chris Holiday—who doesn't exist—and Drex Alister who is almost as much of a ghost."

"I'm not surprised. I knew Drex in high school briefly. He was in and out of foster homes."

"Well, aside from a degree in foreign affairs, he has very little electronic footprint."

Holly's lips quirked. "You don't trust him because he's lacking a social media presence?"

"Even his consulting business is questionable. Just be careful. We don't know much about him."

When the sheriff walked away, he made a bee-line for Janet. With satisfaction, Holly watched him ask her to dance.

"You look amazing."

Warm breath caressed her neck. She spun around to see Drex standing behind her.

"You came." She smiled.

"I said I would." He plucked the drink from her hand and set the two glasses aside.

"I like your tux."

"Do you? It seems I'm a little overdressed for the occasion." He took her hands and led her to the dance floor. "But next to you and your dress, perhaps the tux fits."

"What are we doing?"

He started to sway with her in his arms. She felt evanescent in his embrace as she danced with him.

"I've been waiting a half hour for a break in your socializing. If I'm going to get time to myself, there's no better place than the dance floor."

She smiled at the thought that he was too much of a gentleman to interrupt her as she talked to friends and townspeople.

"For Pete's sake, Holly, will you shut up already so we can go home? You never stop talking to people."

She shrugged off the memory, determined to let nothing detract from this moment.

Drex held Holly in his arms as they floated on the dance floor. He'd barely sipped his champagne, and yet his head buzzed with the magic of Christmas and dancing with a beautiful woman.

He had arrived with his plan still firmly in his mind—Holly would set him up with someone, and he'd be cordial. Then, he felt the magic of the holidays bundled in this beautiful room with the lights, the shining townspeople, the expansive dance floor, and the Christmas music. He talked with people he knew and didn't know—all welcoming him and wishing him happiness. He didn't want to just be cordial; he wanted to relax and be himself —not on another mission.

Holly had appeared in a stunning red dress with her blonde curls twirling over her shoulders. She wore silver earrings and matching silver heels with rhinestones. She looked like Christmas itself. As he watched her smile beaming while she talked to people, he remembered the way she'd welcomed him his first days here and walked arm and arm down Main Street. She was the only woman he wanted to dance with—maybe for the rest of his life, even if that made no rational sense.

Now, he whirled her in his arms as she positively glowed.

"I made an offer on the bookstore," he said.

Her beautiful blue eyes widened. "You did? That's wonderful. Can you swing the shop beside it to add your coffee shop? It's a brilliant idea."

"That's the plan."

"I'll come every day and buy an espresso. Maybe carve out a little place to get work done for an hour or so before I go in to the office."

Silent Night ended, and *Jingle Bell Rock* played. They danced faster as the floor grew more crowded. Soon, they had inadvertently separated as the dance floor became one large conglomeration of people moving and swaying —a partnerless swarm.

He worked his way back to Holly just as *Baby, It's Cold Outside* starting playing. He took her back into his arms.

"I feel like we should end the evening roasting chestnuts on an open fire," he said.

"Oh, I just fixed my fireplace."

"Is that an invitation?"

She bit her lip. "My place is a mess. I mean, I'm not a messy person, but I'm doing a lot of repairs."

"I don't mind. I'd invite you to my fireplace, but it's gas and closed in—not ideal for roasting." And part of him wanted to see inside her house—another glimpse into Holly's life.

If it was anything like the back porch he'd seen at a distance, he would be tempted to offer to pay to fix it, but he couldn't let himself do that. She might take his offer as an offensive gesture that he didn't think she could do it herself.

"Okay, my place." Her smile brightened and then faltered.

"Just sitting by the fire. I promise to be a gentleman."

Her cheeks flushed. "I might want a goodnight kiss though, if it isn't too much to ask."

He grinned. "I could agree to that, but I think I should preview what I'm agreeing to."

His arms tightened slightly around her as he drew her nearer. She tilted her head up as he lowered his lips to hers. Soft and sweet but with a hint of passion just below the surface, begging to be released.

He stepped back, dumbstruck. "I can agree to a goodnight kiss."

Eyes wide, she touched fingers to her lips.

"I'll get our coats." He turned and let out a shaky breath.

Drex, you idiot. Her place? This was a terrible idea. He was falling for this woman, and this town. He couldn't let that happen.

Could he?

Wasn't putting down roots like this what he wanted? Except his name hadn't been cleared yet, so he didn't know if or when he'd be forced to violently uproot himself. He couldn't delude himself into thinking he was safe just because a few weeks of normalcy had passed.

He picked up the coats and turned to look for Holly. She made her way through the crowd, talking to people as she went. He leaned against the wall to wait patiently, admiring her natural charisma and social skills.

ZIELINSKI ROLLED the warmer between his hands as he waited outside the town recreational center. He loathed this part of spy work—long waits in cramped, cold cars—especially with the crap motel he'd been attempting to sleep in the last few days. He was living off fast food and poor sleep quality while spending his days trying to avoid frostbite. Rubbing his eyes, he tried to ignore the throbbing around his temples and gnawing sensation in his upper abdomen. He chewed another two antacids.

He watched as a happy couple walked arm-in-arm out of the rec center and through the parking lot. Oh, this was rich. One month out of the business, and Drex Alister was falling over himself for a woman? Had he forgotten all of his training and become complacent so quickly?

Not likely.

Drex was probably playing some angle here. To what end, Zielinski couldn't fathom. What if this blonde chick was an agent? That would complicate the situation.

He scrutinized the pair of them. If she was an agent—with her Barbie smile and dainty stride—then Zielinski was the patron saint of basket-makers. No, this broad was just Drex's next tumble between the sheets.

Unless she was something more significant.

If Zielinski was going to get the drop on Drex, he needed to use every angle he could. Perhaps this woman would be useful. He would continue to tail the two of them and see if she was an exploitable weakness.

Drex and the woman climbed in separate cars, but no goodbye kiss had been exchanged to suggest the night had concluded. He would bet they'd go to the same place—hers or Drex's.

He started his car, instantly grateful for the heat. He hadn't wanted to let it idle and have the exhaust fumes condense on the air and give away his location. Too bad Drex hadn't had the decency to escape somewhere warmer to die.

CHAPTER 8

*H*olly unlocked the door, and Drex followed her inside her house. She turned on the lights on her way to the living room. The bubbly sensation which had built on the dance floor began to decrescendo as she felt self-conscious about a guest in her unfinished home, as if it was somehow a window to her life—an unfinished work in progress.

Then again, whose life wasn't?

Since she wanted to spend more time getting to know Drex, her house seemed like the ideal place. It was a renovator's dream, and nothing about the atmosphere oozed romance.

"Is it always so chilly in here?" he asked.

"The house is drafty."

"Drafty? There are lean-tos that hold better heat."

She chuckled and added tinder under the fireplace logs. "I thought I'd have more work done on the place by now." She started the fire.

"You'll have the satisfaction of a job well done when it is."

"I thought so when I bought it. Now, it's become all-consuming of my time. I think we have a love-hate relationship."

Drex stood behind her and rubbed his hand up and down her arms along her coat. Her body was keenly aware of his proximity.

"Thanks. I don't have chestnuts, but I do have marshmallows."

"I love roasted marshmallows. But first, let's give the fire time to warm up the room."

They sat on the couch, and Drex pulled the throw blanket over her. He kept his distance and looked relaxed despite his formal wear.

"Tell me about why you ran out on your wedding day," he said gently.

"No preamble, huh? Straight to the heavy stuff. Okay. Harry was the perfect man—everyone said so. We were the perfect couple—everyone said so. The longer we were together, the more I saw a darker side of him." She fidgeted with the frayed edges of the blanket. "All little things—criticisms of the way I drove, or talked too much, or acted clumsily. I always brushed them off, even as his words slowly corroded my self-confidence and self-esteem." She pursed her lips. "But we were perfect together—everyone said so."

Drex scooted closer and took her hand. "How bad did it get?"

"Never physical harm, but the threat of danger always lurked—like a shadow—when he was near. Sometimes it was in the way he'd slam a door, just barely missing me or my fingers. Or the time he backed quickly out of the driveway in anger, and I had to jump out of the way." She hesitated, gauging Drex's reaction. His expression was one of concern and interest. "So, after five years together, I stared at myself in the mirror wearing a chiffon, off-the-shoulder, sleeveless, floor-length wedding dress and about to commit to this person for a lifetime. A lifetime of what? Criticism? Domination? Something worse?"

She pushed to her feet, the blanket falling back onto the couch. She stoked the fire, and the warmth filled the room. Drex silently came to stand by her side.

She continued, "I ran. It felt incredibly liberating to take my life back. I haven't seen Harry since. My family was mortified and humiliated. They know where I've been for the last three years, but they've never visited."

"Did you explain to them how toxic he was?"

"I tried a few times over the years *before* my grand exit, but they dismissed my feelings—treated me as if I was overreacting."

"You did the right thing," Drex said.

She turned to look up at him. "My timing could have been better."

"Better late than never." He drew her back into his arms, pressing her back against his chest.

"I haven't dated since. How much do you really get to know someone? How do you know somebody's darker side won't pose a threat? And Harry's came on so subtly I almost let myself be swallowed by it."

Behind her, Drex went very still. Maybe she had

shared too much, but telling another person her experience, fears, and reservations felt cathartic.

"How about those marshmallows?" he said, taking a step back from her.

She turned to look up at him and saw only warmth and compassion—not an ounce of judgment. "Yes, I'll get them."

"Restroom?" he asked.

She grimaced. "The one downstairs doesn't work. Upstairs and to the right, but be careful on the stairs. Stay to the left. There's a loose board on the right. And don't rely on the handrail."

Drex walked up the stairs carefully, needing to distance himself from Holly before he kissed her again. He'd liked kissing her on the dance floor, but he didn't want to take something too fast and fool himself or Holly about where the two of them were heading.

He inspected the area Holly had referred to as a loose board. Ugh. It was actually broken. One misstep and a leg would go right through. This place wasn't safe.

"Holly, this place isn't even to code," he called as he continued to climb. It was straight out of the Tom Hank's movie *The Money Pit*, except Drex wondered if it was worth the trouble of repairing it.

But the house was Holly's pet project. He wouldn't criticize her, but he began to worry about her safety here.

He reached the upstairs bathroom which appeared in good condition. Holly had done a great job in here, and he could see what she was capable of—the blue tones with cherry wood cabinets. He possessed no handyman skills, but he had the urge to help her nonetheless. What would it feel like to lay tile with her? Paint a room? Sand a floor? He could picture her in torn jeans with her hair in some messy updo.

As he washed his hands, he took a hard look at himself in the mirror and ran a hand over trim facial hair. He was failing at his plans to keep his distance. The more time he spent with her, the more time he wanted to spend with her. But he had secrets. And until he resolved his burned status, he wasn't safe to be around.

Her question by the fire had struck him like a heavy-weight knock-out. *How do you know somebody's darker side isn't going to pose a threat?*

When he returned downstairs, Holly had marshmallows at the ready. The room had warmed enough she'd taken her coat off and sat in front of the fire. Watching her glow by the firelight in her red dress stole his breath away. He'd known hiding was only temporary while he formulated a plan; however, now more than ever, he needed to clear his name so he could build a better life.

As he sat down, Holly handed him a skewer with the fluffy white dessert on the tip.

"What do you remember from high school?" she asked.

He thought for a moment. He remembered never fitting in but didn't dwell on it. Even as a teenager, he recognized those years didn't dictate his future, though he had chosen a life of keeping himself closed to others, so perhaps high school had an element of foreshadowing.

"Coach Simon and Elmo," he said.

"Elmo?"

"This kid in PE was always picked on. I came in a few months into the year, so I didn't know anybody. I broke up a bullying in the locker room and finally asked the guy why everybody called him Elmo. Turns out, his parents actually included that in his name. Franklin Elmo Moss. Apparently, everyone knew him as Frank until the first day of PE his senior year when Coach Simon asked what the "E" stood for. Then, the coach continuously called him Elmo. Months of humiliation ensued after that."

"But you helped him."

Drex shrugged. "The other kids didn't mess with him at PE, but I don't think the rest of his days were kind to him. He did alright though. Went to college and became an engineer."

"So, you did make friends in high school." She nudged his elbow playfully.

"Acquaintances." He smiled.

"And after high school?"

"I went to college, then traveled internationally as a consultant." He inwardly cringed at the consultant lie. Opening up about his spy work would demolish the lovely evening they were enjoying. If he was going to spend more time with her, he would need to explain his real career.

Holly's blue eyes had a tropical glow by the firelight. "I envy your travel. I have been working on a list of places I want to visit. Because I'm focused on saving up, I'm doing a lot of this house myself. I'm trying not to dip into my travel savings."

They continued to talk about places he'd been and

places she wanted to go as the minutes and hours slipped by.

Drex stoked the fire as he glanced at his watch. "I had a wonderful time. And I'm going to head back while it's still a gentlemanly hour to leave."

He helped her stand, pulling her into his arms when she was on her feet. "Thank you for sharing tonight with me. And thank you for sharing your past. I owe you the story behind my fresh start, and I promise I will make that a topic for discussion next time we're alone together."

"I look forward to it." She wrapped her arms around him and pressed her lips to his in a slow, deep kiss.

Was this some type of Christmas magic? She tasted like a hint of peppermint, and her lips sent a quake of desire through him.

Drex pulled away, feeling he didn't deserve the affection she so readily gave. "You make saying goodbye difficult. I am leaving now, but we'll pick up where we left off."

She was smiling from ear to ear in an expression of such happiness and adoration that he felt ten feet tall. He walked away, came back, gave her three more kisses in quick succession, and then forced himself to leave.

Ironically, neither of them had been looking for a relationship when they found each other. Now they seemed to be heading that direction.

As soon as he exited her house, the darkness of the winter night closed in around him. Holly had looked so happy. Would he destroy that when he told her the truth about who he was? He didn't want to hurt her, but at this point, it seemed inevitable.

❋

THE NEXT MORNING, Drex checked his email in his pajamas as he sipped coffee. He had one word from Chester's encrypted account: TROUBLE.

He choked on the sip of coffee he'd started taking as his heart plummeted.

Idiot, idiot, idiot.

He was dreaming up plans for a happily ever-after in the arms of a beautiful woman as if he didn't have a bounty on his head. Pipe dreams.

With a lump in his throat, he called Chester, not knowing what country or even what time zone she was in. It could've been the middle of the night for all he knew, but *trouble* wasn't an email title he didn't take lightly.

"Drex?"

"Chester, what trouble?" He held his breath.

"They know where you are," she said, solemnly.

"Who are *they*, exactly?"

"CIA. They sent a hitman."

Even though Drex had considered the possibility, it devastated him to hear it. He took the stairs two at a time and put Chester on speaker as he quickly dressed and thought of the chilling Ernest Hemingway quote:

"There is no hunting like the hunting of man, and those who have hunted men long enough and liked it, never care for anything else thereafter."

Chester continued, "And Zielinski's got enough friends in the organization—if they know, he knows. He hasn't been at the office for a few days, according to Gruber."

A few days? Drex felt nauseated. If he'd been spying on himself—a lot could be learned in a few days. He should have trusted his sense of being watched intermittently and been more careful.

What would Zielinski have seen covertly?

Holly.

If his traitorous ex-boss wanted to make Drex vulnerable, he only needed to go after Holly. After pulling on black slacks, he shrugged on a shirt and buttoned it.

"You're quiet," Chester said. "Usually at this point in the conversation, you would be telling me you're packing, leaving, and activating a new alias."

"I can't cut and run. There's somebody here I care about." He thought about where Holly would be right now. Probably getting ready for the holiday parade she'd mentioned last night.

"How are you going to fix this? You've got the CIA and Zielinski bearing down on you, and an innocent who could get caught in the crossfire."

"The first thing I need to do is tell Holly the truth." He scampered down the stairs and tugged on his boots, followed by lacing them.

"Holly? That's her name?" Chester snorted. "Yes, you definitely need to come clean about your pseudonym. You can't marry her and give her name like Holly Holiday."

"You're a barrel of laughs, Chester," he deadpanned. He slipped his gun into his holster, zipped up his coat, and headed out into the cold. "You'll call me if you get wind of anything else?"

"I will."

Drex pocketed his phone and walked to Main Street where he was surprised to see the elbow to elbow crowd along both sides of the road—tourists and townsfolk both ready to watch the parade. One by one, trucks pulling floats drove slowly down the road with music playing from loudspeakers. He suspected the weather was cold for a marching band.

The first float looked like something out of Candy Land, with marshmallows hanging from pink trees, life-size candy canes sticking out of gum drops large enough to sit on, and a giant gingerbread house. The second float had a blue and white castle with twinkling lights. After the winter wonderland came a float with the outline of a train brilliantly lit with hundreds of colored lights.

The fourth float was Santa's sleigh. Sheriff Carpenter, decked out in a full red velvet suit, shiny black boots, and a Santa hat, waved to the crowd. Beside him, Holly-the-elf smiled and waved. There was no way the elf outfit was warm enough for the weather, and Drex felt the urge to haul her back to the fireside and wrap the blanket around her again.

The final float was a giant Christmas tree with shiny red and green presents—boxes large enough for people to fit inside. The unnerving tingling sensation of being watched returned. He scanned the crowd but saw no one watching him or standing out in the crowd.

He worked his way down the sidewalk where a toddler fought his mother's grip as she was turned toward her middle child who seemed to be arguing with her mother about something. The toddler squirmed with all his might, face wrinkled in determination as his tiny gloved hand slipped through his mother's fingers.

Free at last, he wobbled in his little boots, stiff in his heavy winter coat. Then, he turned and ran, face gleeful from his hard-earned freedom but oblivious to the large tire of the float bearing down on him.

Having predicted the projected path of the boy, Drex was already in motion. When he broke through the crowd, he dropped to his knees, the momentum sliding him across ice and snow.

He scooped up the child as he spun away from the vehicle before bringing them both to a halt when he dug his boot in the snow.

The woman gasped, and the boy giggled at the ride. Drex offered him up to her.

"You saved him!" Tears welled in her eyes as a small group of people gaped at Drex.

He stood and brushed snow off his pants. "No problem," he murmured.

"Wait. Let me thank you."

But he was already disappearing into the crowd. In spy work, drawing attention to oneself was an occupational hazard. The spotlight and a sniper's crosshairs could be one and the same. He didn't want anyone's praise or recognition.

When the parade ended, people disbursed inside the shops along Main Street—the bakery, the bookstore, the bistro. Regardless of their destinations, people sought warmth. Drex walked down to the recreation center where the Santa float had parked. That must be where they were holding Santa's Workshop and visitation.

By the time he reached the inside, a line of anxious children and equally jittery parents, ready with their camera phones, stretched to the door. At the beginning of the line was the North Pole with Santa and his elf.

Drex hung back. Nothing untoward would happen to Holly in a public place such as this. But if Zielinski and the CIA knew Drex's location, he might catch them in the act of spying. Drex vigilantly observed, hoping to glimpse the watchers watching.

He didn't see Zielinski's broad body, nor anyone acting suspiciously. When the line ended, Holly disappeared to the back toward the restroom where Drex suspected she would change before heading home. He would wait for her there, walk her to her car, and explain the situation.

"Hi. I'm a burned spy who has put you in danger by association. Do you still want to date?"

Hmm. Maybe he should work the kinks out of his speech first.

As he headed in Holly's direction, a large figure stepped between him and his destination.

He blinked at the gleaming red suit and fluffy hat. "Sheriff Carpenter." He tried to keep the irritation out of his voice.

The sheriff removed his Santa hat. "I think it's time you and I had a chat, Drex Alister."

CHAPTER 9

" **H** appy to oblige, after I see Holly home safe," Drex told Sheriff Carpenter.

"Holly has been seeing herself home just fine for the last three years in this town. I'm sure she'll manage." He gave Drex a curt smile that, with his Santa suit on, made Drex feel like he'd made the naughty list.

Perhaps he had—between losing an informant in Prague, getting burned, having his new identity crumble, and potentially involving a woman in his danger. The last month had been a series of unfortunate events culminating in inevitable disaster.

Drex grit his teeth but didn't argue. He didn't want to make a scene at the rec center with the sheriff in front of families. He sensed that if he resisted, the sheriff intended to use force. If he truly was going to make a fresh start in this town, assaulting the sheriff—especially with him dressed like Santa in a room full of children—would be counterproductive to those goals. He detested the idea of leaving Holly alone, but a showdown with the sheriff wouldn't land him any closer to her. The best he could hope for was that his cooperation would speed this interaction along.

Drex walked side-by-side with the sheriff, back out into the cold. "What's this about?"

"Let's get toasty indoors. We can talk more over a cup of coffee." There was nothing friendly or 'toasty' about the sheriff's invitation for coffee, and Drex suspected this conversation would take place in the sheriff's office, not the bistro.

Joe Carpenter would want to have this discussion on his territory. Whether the intention was to intimidate Drex or because the sheriff feared what Drex might do in a confrontation, Drex wasn't sure. He'd been in enough tight spots and tense situations that being questioned in a small-town sheriff's office wouldn't phase him. But angst gnawed at his insides when he thought about how he was leaving Holly unguarded in the wake of this morning's news from Chester. Danger was already closing in on him and could spill over into her life.

As they walked down Main Street, Drex wondered if the sheriff would go so far as to frisk him. If he did, he would find his gun, and although Drex had a license to carry a concealed weapon—as Chris Holiday—he suspected such a discovery would only lengthen his time away from Holly.

When they reached the sheriff's office, Carpenter pulled open the door and let Drex enter first. "Come on and have a seat by my desk over there."

The entire office consisted of three desks in the small hallway leading to a back room, presumably where a jail cell might be—just one, judging by the overall size of the building. A deputy sat in uniform, typing on his computer.

Drex left his coat buttoned to keep his gun concealed as he sat. "What has you concerned, Sheriff?"

Sheriff Carpenter pulled off his Santa coat, beneath which was a taupe-colored long-sleeve shirt. He adjusted the badge on his belt before sitting down. "I don't like strangers with strange identities nesting in my town. I heard Holly call you Drex Alister in the bistro a while back after you clearly identified yourself to me as Chris Holiday. Turns out, Drex Alister is a bit of a ghost. Foster homes here and there, and then off the grid. For a decade."

Drex pursed lips. He would have to take a gamble that telling the truth was the most direct route to getting protection on Holly. The sheriff hadn't arrested him yet or surrounded him with men, which meant he didn't know Drex was wanted by the CIA. He didn't know the US government suspected Drex of foul play and the assassination of a Czech citizen planning to defect.

"The reason I don't have a traceable history in the last ten years is that I am... I was a spy."

"What are you telling me? That you're CIA?"

Drex suppressed an eye roll. Why did everyone assume American spy equaled CIA? There were dozens of private spy agencies, the sum of which outnumbered the Central Intelligence Agency's number of officers doing covert field work.

"No. Not CIA. A private organization. Sometimes I did work for the CIA. In November, I was double-crossed during an information transfer. I came here in hiding with a new identity because I made the reasonable assumption that the person who double-crossed me would like to silence me. Permanently."

"Why would this person want to silence you?" the sheriff asked.

"That's classified. However, we have a more immediate, concerning problem. I learned just this morning that the crooked spy has identified my new nesting spot." He chose the sheriff's term for emphasis.

He also suspected the sheriff's digging was what alerted the CIA to Drex's new home, but he wasn't going to win the man over by pointing out that his curiosity probably facilitated endangering Holly. After all, Drex was ultimately the one to blame after spending so much time with her.

"You're going to stick with this line of answers? That you're a spy?"

"I'll give you an example. Reginald, the banker is having an affair."

"Everybody knows that. He's seeing Julie Taylor."

"Yes. And her daughter."

The sheriff's eyes went wide. "She's only eighteen."

"Yes. Not a healthy situation. And Mrs. Rice is stealing money from the bistro tip jar."

Sheriff Carpenter grunted.

"And the Matthews kid is your firebug."

He raised an eyebrow at Drex.

"You've been looking for who has been starting fires in the woods. At least, I assume so based on the newspaper articles."

"So why did you go to a Christmas parade? If you're

some super spy with people after you, shouldn't you be moving onto the next town?" Carpenter leaned back and crossed his arms, clearly not willing to entertain the idea that an urgency existed to the situation.

"Because I suspect he'll go after Holly to get to me."

"And that's why you've been following Holly around all morning like a stalker?"

Drex wondered if his behavior this morning had been what prompted the sheriff to act on his desire to confront Drex. "Yes. And now she's unguarded because I'm here."

Carpenter regarded him but didn't move.

"Can I go now?" The worry in Drex's chest that had started like an ache now became a tight band.

"It's quite a story you've concocted."

"It's the truth."

"Could be. Could be you're delusional, and you're the real threat to Holly."

"I'm not delusional."

Sheriff Carpenter stood and came around the desk. "Be that as it may," he withdrew a pair of handcuffs and slapped them on Drex's left wrist while simultaneously connecting him to the chair, "I'm going let you hang out here until we get some answers."

Drex looked at the handcuffs in disbelief. "Seriously? Are you arresting me, because I haven't heard my rights yet."

"I'm considering arresting you."

"On what charges?"

"We'll start with possession of a fake ID—I'm sure your driver's license says Chris Holiday—and then we will see what else crops up. The only reason I'm not throwing you in the cell this very instant is that I saw you save Molly's little boy from the float. Man who'd do that deserves one chance to prove himself. One." With unhurried motions, the sheriff walked back around his desk and picked up his brown fur-lined wool coat. As he pulled it on, he looked toward the deputy across the room at his desk. "Ned, please keep an eye on our guest."

"You're making a mistake, Joe," Drex said. His voice held an edge of plea rather than a threat, but that didn't seem to faze the sheriff.

The white bearded man gave him one last hard look before leaving.

HOLLY ARRIVED HOME, humming Christmas songs. She'd seen Drex at the parade and Santa's workshop. He looked strained, but perhaps his tension had been because of the cold weather. He'd vanished when she'd looked for him after she changed, but she decided she would call him later.

She'd felt light as a feather dancing in Drex's arms last night, and the effervescent sensation lingered after he'd left her house. When she'd finally fallen asleep, it was after midnight. The next morning, she'd dressed and gone to the parade, thinking only of the next time she could see him.

Starving after the parade and workshop, she popped a bagel in the toaster.

Figgy appeared in the kitchen, floating above the counter. She hadn't seen him since before the party.

"Figgy McJingle! Magic was in the air last night. Did you see it? Could you feel it?"

"You found your match / he's quite the catch."

"I could've danced all night. I could've talked all night. I could've been convinced into doing some other things last night, too, but it would've been too fast. It already feels fast. But in a good way. Does that make sense?" She smeared hazelnut cream cheese on the bagel.

"Both of you were glowing / but I am not all knowing."

"Figgy, did you see what he did in front of the float? He saved that toddler—just whooshed in with no thought for his own safely and like he saw the whole thing coming."

She puzzled, picturing the event in her mind. "You don't think he has someone like you? A ghost who fore-warned him about the child?" She took a bite of her bagel.

"He sees no ghosts / but there's no time to boast." His small brow wrinkled in worry. "Danger has arrived in town."

Holly let out a disbelieving chuckle. "Danger? What danger? In Blitzen?"

"Dangerous men are coming 'round." Figgy's small, worried voice sent a chill down her spine.

"The cards are cast / Drex has a past. You'll have to be strong / to write the wrong. He'll need your help too / if your feelings are true."

Holly looked down at the unfinished bagel. "What are you talking about in his past, and what 'wrong'? My feel-ings are true. What am I supposed to do?" Ugh. He had her rhyming again.

But he also had her genuinely worried. If Drex needed

her help, she would help. What was Figgy trying to tell her? Maybe Drex would need her help but not think he could ask for it. Hmm. She might suspect an unwilling-ness to ask for help from a man in a tux. Oh, that tux. Her knees went watery again.

"Figgy, as clearly as you can, tell me what I need to do to help Drex."

"Big man with big hands / don't try to make a stand. Grab your keys with the scare / retreat to the stairs."

"I'll call Drex." She could clear up this whole danger-looming nonsense by talking to Drex. She snatched up her phone and dialed his number. As it rang—and rang and rang—she poured herself a large glass of water and quenched her parched throat.

"No answer," she told the elf ghost as worry pricked along her skin.

A knock came at the door, causing her to jump, and her heart thudded against her chest. If Figgy hadn't mentioned danger, she would think nothing of a visitor and readily open the door. Instead, she stood paralyzed.

Had she locked the door? Yes, she remembered. But it was an old door that wouldn't withstand someone deter-mined to get in the house, someone dangerous.

Dangerous men are coming 'round.

She looked at Figgy who shook his head in warning. She took his motion as an indication that Drex wasn't the person knocking at her door.

She crept silently to the front door to where her boots rested and slipped them on.

Another bang, bang, bang. "Miss Sanders, I know you're in there. We need to talk about Drex Alister."

As she grabbed her coat and keys, she glimpsed the silhouette of the man on the other side of the door. The big man, as Figgy had described him.

"Miss Sanders?"

Without answering, she backed away slowly.

A loud clatter resounded through the house as the front door cracked violently and swung open on its hinges.

Holly let out a yelp and retreated toward the stairs. A gunshot rang so loud she thought it might have shattered her eardrum. Wood splintered in the banister to her left where the bullet struck.

She froze one third of the way up the stairs. Shaking, she turned around to face the gunman.

He wore a brown overcoat over his large torso. Salt and pepper hair covered his head, framing a square face with drooping jowls. His eyes were a cold, eerie calm—deceptive and deadly as black ice.

"I just want to talk, Miss Sanders."

"My door and your gun would suggest otherwise." She tried to calm her tremulous body. She'd never heard a gunshot in her life, much less been shot at.

"You could have opened the door. You didn't, which means you already suspect trouble. Did Alister tell you he's on the run from the CIA? Or did he feed you lies? I'm one of the good guys, Miss Sanders. Come down, and I'll explain everything over a cup of coffee."

"He told me everything," she lied. She took a cautious step backward up the stairs, thinking of Figgy's words—*don't try to make a stand.*

"Don't take another step, or the next bullet goes in you."

"Not something one of the good guys would say," she pointed out in a high-pitched voice. And this man obviously wanted her alive to use against Drex, which meant Figgy was right, and running away was her best option.

Her only option.

She bolted up and into the master bedroom. Behind her, the man cursed and started up the stairs. When she heard a crash, she knew he'd planted a foot onto and through the loose board.

That would buy her a little time. She pulled on her coat and stuffed the keys in her pocket. She opened the master bedroom sliding glass door that led to the deck—the rickety, crooked deck with rotting boards that she hadn't replaced yet.

Gingerly, she picked her way across the wood to the brittle railing. Below, a snowdrift had piled against her shed. It would be the softest place to land. She kicked boards out of way. As she stared at the drop below, her nerve faltered.

Jump, jump, jump. She silently repeated the words, but her body didn't move.

Footsteps up the stairs resumed. No time for anything else. She pushed off the deck. For a moment, she was flying. Fear made her stomach flip and her whole body tensed for impact. In a poof of white powder, she landed in the soft snow and sank to her waist.

"Stop!" the angry man shouted.

Holly looked up in time to see him stomp out onto the deck.

Your mistake, big guy.

The entire structure shimmied, and he couldn't aim his gun as he tried to maintain his balance.

Holly waded through the snow, agonizingly slower than she would have liked, as her pursuer wobbled precariously on the deck.

Once she'd freed herself from the snow pile, she dashed for her car. As she climbed inside, snow from her clothes poofed in a flurry of white, coating her seats and dashboard. She started the engine, backed out, and reached the road.

"Figgy, where is Drex?" Her voice came in rapid pants as she gripped the steering wheel with white-knuckled fear.

He appeared beside her. "Go to his house / you'll meet a mouse. The truth is there / but do take care."

"A mouse?" She shook her head in exasperation.

She tried asking Figgy for more information as they drove, but he only gave her more riddles.

When she pulled into Drex's driveway, his car wasn't there.

She turned and blinked at Figgy. "Now what?"

"Knock on the door / the truth you'll explore."

As she walked toward the door, her heart rate crept higher. Over the course of the drive here, the relentless pounding had finally subsided since jumping off her back deck. Warily, she walked up the steps and knocked on the door.

A tall, lean man, ten years older than Drex answered the door. He wore a navy suit that enhanced his predatorial features—high cheeks, narrow nose, sharp eyes. "You must be Holly. My name is Spinner."

CHAPTER 10

*D*rex surveyed the sheriff's office for a second time. Handcuffs weren't a problem, but he didn't want to hurt the deputy. Although Sheriff Carpenter didn't believe his spy story, he seemed to worry that Holly could be in real danger. Drex hoped that meant the next place Carpenter would go was Holly's house. He'd feel better knowing the sheriff was checking on her safety.

Except, the sheriff wasn't a match for a CIA hitman, nor Zielinski. Neither of them would have much reservation about eliminating the sheriff and would probably turn the blame on Drex.

"Bathroom break?" he asked Ned, starting to stand.

The deputy shook his head as he continued to type on his computer. The work looked like some type of mundane data entry. Drex lowered himself back down, discretely pulling a paperclip off the sheriff's desk.

He made quick work of releasing the cuffs, the slight

metallic noise inaudible to the deputy over the sounds of Christmas music playing in the room.

As he let the handcuffs fall, Drex whipped out his gun and pointed it at the deputy. The man looked up at him, stunned and terrified without even having time to reach for his own weapon.

"Up, slowly. My apologies for this, Ned, but I need to make sure Holly is safe."

The deputy rose tentatively, hands raised in the air.

"Two fingers, gun out, and set it on the desk."

He did as he was instructed.

"Walk around and down the hall to the jail." Drex followed Ned, gun still trained on him. "Door open. You step in, toss me the keys, and close the door."

Ned hesitated, as if considering a counterattack.

"If your wondering if you're fast enough, you're not," Drex said.

After Ned reluctantly stepped inside the cell, Drex locked the door. Next, he holstered his weapon and dashed for the front door where a blast of cold wind struck him. He took off at a sprint, boots crunching on snow.

He would have to go to his house first to get his car and then drive to Holly's place. He pulled out his phone as he ran and saw he had a missed call from her. He couldn't decide if that made him feel better or worse about whether or not trouble had reached her.

He was about to call her back when he turned the corner onto Pine Street and saw her car parked in his drive. Once again, he didn't know if this was a good thing or a bad thing.

He continued his dash... *through the snow*. He could have laughed at the irony if he wasn't weighted with worry.

When he reached the front porch, he pulled out his gun again. He listened for a minute as he caught his breath. People were talking inside his house. Holly's voice. She sounded like her usual bubbly self and not in any distress. The ache in his chest eased slightly.

Who was she talking to? Was she on her phone? And how had she gotten inside his house? She had returned the spare key.

He unlocked the door and opened it, leading with his gun as he entered. He risked scaring the daylight out of Holly with his weapon, but he didn't want to take any chances with her safety in the event he was entering a dangerous situation.

When Drex reached his living room, he saw Holly sitting on his recliner and CIA officer Stan Spinner on his couch. From what he could tell, Drex was the only one holding a weapon. That didn't make Stan any less of a threat.

He was a known killer in the spy business.

CURSING, Zielinski brushed off snow and limped from Holly's backyard to his car. He'd sprained an ankle and just about threw out his shoulder when the piece of junk deck came crashing down. To make matters worse, Barbie escaped—car and all.

She would probably run to her boyfriend, which

would alert Drex Alister to his presence. The pair of them would have a good ten minutes' head start, so he may not catch up to them.

When a police cruiser pulled into the drive behind his car, Zielinski was relieved he'd holstered his weapon out of sight before leaving Holly's backyard.

He held up his credentials for the sheriff to see. "Glad you're here, sheriff. I'm Victor Zielinski. I work with the CIA."

The sheriff, as broad as himself, sported a generous white beard. He kept one hand on the pistol on his waist as he approached and took Zielinski's cred pack. He sized him up as any good law enforcement would do—probably noticing Zielinski's rough appearance, as though he'd been mauled by a bear.

"This says you're in private security." He handed the cred pack back to Zielinski.

He pocketed it. "That's right. I'm looking for a rogue agent who used to work for me. Name's Drex Alister, though I suspect he would be using one of his many aliases since he's in hiding." Zielinski opted to skirt as close to the truth as he could, since he didn't know how much the sheriff had already unearthed.

"Mr. Alister doesn't live here."

"No, sir. He wasn't at his place, so I tried the woman's home whom I saw him with earlier. She's not home either." He gave him a disarming smile.

The sheriff hiked his pants up around his waist. "Mr. Alister is in my custody at present."

"Oh, good. That's better for the safety of this town." Zielinski tried to keep his smile from turning into clenched teeth. He couldn't eliminate Drex in front of the sheriff, not easily anyway. And after too many nights in a crappy motel with a clunky heater, days of cold exposure in his vehicle, and falling to injury on a busted deck, he desperately wanted to shoot Drex.

"Why don't you ride with me? We'll go speak with him together."

Zielinski wanted to recoil at the very idea of riding in some hick's car and being stuck at the sheriff's department without his own vehicle, especially if he needed to make a quick getaway after eliminating Drex, but he needed to appear cooperative if the sheriff was going to trust him to spend time with Drex, or even let him take the ex-spy into custody.

"Thank you. Great idea."

They climbed into the cruiser, and the sheriff backed out of Holly's driveway.

"I'm glad you have him contained. He's a danger to society."

The sheriff cast him a sideways glance.

"Killed a man in the Czech republic," Zielinski added. He resisted the urge to rub at the rising burning sensation in his stomach. His antacids were back in his vehicle.

"That so?"

"It's a CIA matter, so I can't go into the details."

"I understand."

The sheriff's phone rang, and he answered it, putting the call on speaker. "Ned, I'm here with someone who used to work with Drex Alister. We're on our way to you now."

"He got away!" The man on the other end of the line shouted.

"What?"

"He got out of the cuffs, pulled a gun on me, and got away."

When Sheriff Carpenter looked at him, Zielinski pursed his lips as if to say this turn of events emphasized how dangerous he'd been telling the sheriff Alister was.

"Are you hurt?" the sheriff asked Ned.

"I'm okay. He locked me in the jail cell, but I still had my phone on me."

"He's on foot?"

"I think so. Didn't take any of our keys."

"Then I'll head to his place. He'd go there first for his vehicle."

"What about me?" Ned asked.

"If he didn't take any keys, then you have the jail keys there?"

"Yeah, but I can't get to them."

"You have your phone, Ned. Call someone who'll let you out. Maybe pick someone who won't blab to the town about how the deputy got locked in his own jail cell." He disconnected the call.

When the sheriff took the next hard right, Zielinski wanted to shout with glee. If Drex was at his house instead of the sheriff's office, the less controlled situation with fewer witnesses could prove to be the perfect situation. He could eliminate Drex, maybe the sheriff, too, since the white-bearded man seemed a little too savvy for his own good.

If he rigged the scene correctly, he could make it look

like Drex killed the sheriff. Then, he could take Drex's car back to Holly's house, reclaim his car, leave town, and no one would be the wiser.

"Drex!"

Drex regarded her wide, albeit somewhat tentative smile, but kept his gun trained on Spinner.

Holly stood but didn't approach Drex. "I would give you a hug, but you look a little scary right now."

"You're not hurt?"

"No." She shook her head.

Drex wanted to get closer to her, but he couldn't lower his guard with Spinner twenty feet away. "Stan, you're looking well." His kept his voice cool.

"Alister, Merry Christmas." Stan remained very still, as if wanting to demonstrate to Drex that he wasn't a threat, but Drex knew what a man like Stan was capable of doing. He could go from zero to sixty before Drex had a chance to shoot him down.

"It's okay, Drex," Holly said. "Stan explained how you used to be a spy, and how you got out when Zielinski double-crossed you. Stan is here for the intel from Prague."

Drex cocked his head to one side and regarded Holly. She was accepting of all this? His distrusting, spy mentality wondered for a moment if she was somehow part of this—a plant to deceive him—but that was impossible. He dismissed the thought almost as quickly as it occurred.

He noted some scrapes on her hand and one across her cheek, just enough that they were tiny streaks of red.

"Are you hurt?" he asked again.

"No." She shook her head. "But I did meet your former boss. Zielinski claimed he wanted to talk, but he did more shooting than talking."

Shooting? Drex's stomach knotted. Holly had been in danger because of him.

"Alister," Stan interjected, "we only have part of Ludvik's intel, and we have reason to believe he gave you the other part. Let me take the information you have back to Langley. Let me clear your name."

"Why do you believe I'm innocent?"

Stan hadn't threatened Holly and hadn't taken any action to stage his own house before Drex arrived. Maybe he did believe Drex was innocent.

Stan slowly stood. "A guilty man who sabotages a mission for financial gain does not proceed to help the defector's family out of the country for safety. Those were not the actions of a self-serving spy."

"How did you know that?" Drex asked in surprise.

"You saved my life, Alister. Maybe Amsterdam was just another day on the job for you. But I would've died if you hadn't risked your life to take the extra time to save me. When I was assigned to your case after Prague, I knew they had misinformation. I used a few connections and dug a little deeper. I've been watching you for the last week, and then watching Zielinski watching you. So here we are. Can you put the gun away?"

Drex recalled the Amsterdam incident. He'd been there to retrieve information from a former Irish Republican Army fanatic at a building that was going to be bombed by Turkish terrorists. Stan was being held captive there. When Drex learned about the American, he made a brief off-the-books side mission. He didn't do more than incapacitate two guards and an interrogator and pack Stan into a taxi, but apparently, he'd made an impression.

Drex holster his gun. "Do you know where Zielinski is now?"

Holly looked like she wanted to hug to Drex, but the slightest reservation hovered in her expression. She must have seen the way he looked at her just for an instant, as if she was part of the conspiracy against him.

He walked toward her. "Holly, I'm so sorry for dragging you into this and putting you in harm's way." He wrapped his arms around her.

Thankfully, she returned the embrace. "I'm okay. Shocked, but okay. Last I saw Zielinski, he was teetering on my deck."

Keeping one arm around Holly, Drex disconnected the tiny USB from his watch and handed it to Stan. He had this copy he'd made from the phone download at Letná Park. "I didn't want to part with it until I could be sure it would be in the right hands. Whatever is on there, it cost a man his life."

Stan nodded solemnly as he accepted it.

A loud knock sounded at the door. "Mr. Alister, it's Sheriff Carpenter. I'm here with Victor Zielinski."

"We can take off out the back," Stan suggested in a whisper.

Drex squeezed Holly closer. "This is my home. You get

that information in the right hands. I'll answer to the sheriff."

Stan gave him a grateful nod before disappearing toward the back of the house.

"Drex?" the sheriff called again.

"Yes. I'm in here with Holly. We're going to open the door."

"Holly, you're okay?"

"I'm fine. We're both fine in here," she called out without leaving Drex's side.

He would have preferred meeting the men without Holly there, but Sheriff Carpenter needed to know she was safe since her car was parked outside. Drex could only hope Zielinski wouldn't try anything rash with the sheriff present. Still, he shifted his weight to feel the gun in his holster.

Slowly, and with Holly tucked in by his side, he opened the door. The two men standing in the cold glared at him. Zielinski, looking surprisingly strung out, made Drex wonder if any of his haggard appearance was the result of a guilty conscience.

"Zielinski," he greeted him curtly without inviting him inside his house. "You look like you got run over by a reindeer. I would introduce Holly, but she tells me the two of you already met."

The sheriff gave a slight arch to his eyebrow as he kept one hand on his gun handle.

"You're burned, Alister," Zielinski spat. "You need to give up information the government paid to have delivered—the secrets you stole."

Drex moved his body ever so slightly, partially in front

of Holly. He didn't like Zielinski's bloodshot eyes and twitching left temple. He looked like a man on the edge.

"Those secrets are safely in the hands of the CIA. Did you know they sent Spinner after me? Fortunately, I saved his life in Amsterdam—I left that tidbit out of my report as it didn't seem relevant to the mission. I'm happy that piece of karma worked in my favor. With a little more good fortune, the CIA will find out who actually ordered the hit on Ludvik and work to clear my name."

Zielinski's face contorted in a snarl as he reached for his weapon.

A shot rang out.

CHAPTER 11

*H*olly jolted at the sound of yet another gunshot. As it happened, Drex turned toward her and wrapped his arms around her.

With her ears ringing, she frisked him. "You're okay. You're not shot." She couldn't see around Drex, but she could hear the other man screaming.

"No. I'm fine. The sheriff shot Zielinski in the hand."

She held tight to Drex, but turned him slightly so she could see the sheriff. "Joe, you're okay?"

"I'm fine, Holly. You stay inside. I'm going to call for an ambulance and Ned." With a glare at Drex, he added. "Assuming he's managed to get out of the jail cell."

As the sheriff confiscated Zielinski's abandoned gun on the porch, Drex let go of Holly long enough to fetch a towel from the kitchen and toss it to his former boss for his hand. The sheriff called in the incident.

When he finished, Drex asked him, "How did you know I was innocent?"

"Had a hunch. I didn't trust you at first. I got worried when Holly was growing attached, even though she's a good judge of character. Your coming clean in my office helped, albeit it seemed a bit far-fetched, until this unscrupulous gentleman made an appearance." He cast a disparaging look at Zielinski who lay on the porch clutching his wrapped hand.

Drex turned toward Holly. "I'm sorry I wasn't honest about who I was. I should have told you sooner."

"I'm still processing it, but I'm glad you're okay."

"I was terrified something bad was going to happen to you."

When he buried his face in her hair by her neck, she startled. His expression of vulnerability rendered her momentarily speechless.

"Did you mean what you said about this being your home?" she asked.

He pulled back and looked down at her with a smile. "This house, this town, and you. It's all my home."

TWO DAYS LATER

"Lot's of big events, Figgy." Holly paced her living room as she tugged at the sleeves of her sweater. "I'm seeing Drex tonight. And on Christmas day, my family is driving down for a day visit."

She had called her family the day after her brush with death—both getting shot at and jumping off her porch.

She didn't tell her parents any of those events, but she did ask them over for Christmas lunch. To her surprise, they agreed to come and seemed genuinely excited about the invitation. It was past time for them all to reconcile.

Her living room and kitchen were in decent enough shape for company, and the downstairs bathroom was functional now. She covered the bullet hole in her second-floor indoor balcony with twinkling garland, which she also looped over the front of the stairs so no guests would attempt to go up them and suffer injury.

"Your life is an orderly shelf / you've no more need for this elf."

She stopped and stared at him. "You're leaving?" Technically, she was supposed to have one more day before he vanished, but she suspected he meant goodbye for good, not just this Christmas.

"To others I must gesture / this concludes our adventure."

"I guess part of me suspected I couldn't have you forever. You've been wonderful. You helped a lot of people these last three Christmases, but mostly me. I'm grateful."

"Your happiness is my reward / Pass the candle to a new steward."

"I promise. Thank you for everything. I'll never forget you."

With tears in her eyes, she watched Figgy McJingle's small form grow more translucent before disappearing all together with one last jingle noise from his hat.

❄

Drex opened the door and let Holly in out of the cold. She took off her boots, hat, and coat in the entrance. He had cleaned his porch of all traces of the incident with his former boss.

"Merry Christmas." He leaned in and kissed her cheek.

After the Zielinski incident, he'd spent hours answering the sheriff's questions, followed by a debriefing with the CIA. He'd had to wait until today to see Holly, and he'd spent the time apart, unsure of what she thought of everything she'd learned about him.

"Merry Christmas." She beamed a smile at him that made him think a relationship with her could work.

"I made Cornish hens, stuffed bell peppers, and side salads."

"You've been busy." She followed him into the kitchen. "And it smells amazing."

"Do you like wine? I have red or white. I have champagne, but I planned on saving that for when you come over for New Year's."

"Am I coming over for New Year's?"

"A guy can hope." He pulled out the wine opener.

"I don't have any plans. I could be convinced."

He turned toward her. "What sort of convincing do you require?"

"Well. I'm a hugger. So, if we want to try this dating thing, I need a hug every time we see each other."

He set down the wine opener, slid over to her, and wrapped his arms around her. "I can definitely do that. I wanted to hold you in my arms the minute I opened the door, but I didn't want to be too forward—especially since I don't know how you feel about my past."

She looked up at him, eyes dancing. "It's definitely unconventional. And I get that there will be things you can't tell me and things I don't want to know. I've seen your true nature—looking out for me, saving Stan's life, saving Molly's toddler. Your actions tell me you're one of the good guys. And you are going to be the most amazing travel guide. I have to bring you on all of my trips."

He laughed. "I can accommodate that. Minus a few countries I should probably never go back to."

"Hmm. Oh, and I think you should have one little section of your bookstore dedicated to spy novels—just for the irony."

"I like that."

"Oh, and you should have your own spy novel. *The Spy Who Saved Christmas*. Or maybe *The Spy Who Loved Me*—no, that one is taken. *The Spy of Blitzen*—which is funny since it sounds intense, but it actually takes place in small town Maryland."

"How about *The Spy Who Found Christmas*. I came to this town claiming I was making a fresh start when I intended to avoid people and entanglements like I always do. You changed that, Holly. Because of you, life has the potential to be better than I ever imagined. Maybe the title should be *The Spy Who Kissed Holly*. And, maybe it's too soon to say something like this, but I'm falling in love with you."

She arched up to him, and he met her with a kiss. The delightful connection was slow and sensual as it shattered all the worry he'd harbored that his past would change how she felt about him. He didn't think he deserved this woman's affection, but he could spend every moment with her earning it.

When the kiss ended, she whispered into his ear, "It's not too soon."

CAROL'S CHRISTMAS

One night.
Two hearts.
Three spirits.

A new twist on a Christmas classic. Over the course of the night, three ghosts visit bitter surgeon, Carol Sullivan, causing her to reconsider the choices she's made and the person she's become. But can she truly make the difficult transformation or is compassion--and love--lost forever?

CHAPTER 1

"She's going to die." Tony Olsen paced the small office in the back of the pawnshop.

"Relax. Everybody dies, Tony." Burke took a drag off of the cigarette that perpetually hung from his bottom lip. "I mean, look at the pair of us—a couple of nobody ghosts who don't want to move on."

Tony ran a hand through his gray hair. "But I've seen her death, Burke. Christmas morning. Bam!" He smacked his hands together. "Hit by a delivery truck. A truck!"

He'd watched the vision of Carol's death in slow motion. She walked toward the curb, distracted and not checking traffic. She stepped off into the road, and the truck that hit her didn't have time to slow down, or even swerve.

"There's a lot of tragedy in this world, Tony. She's lived to be forty-two—that's a lot more than some people get."

Burke leaned back in his chair. The chair didn't move

or squeak beneath his weight, and there was no noise even as he clumped his feet up onto the office desk.

"Besides," he continued, "from what you've told me about this woman, she don't got much of a life nowadays as it is."

Tony shoved his hands in his slacks—his Giorgio Armani suit pants. They were the very ones he'd been buried in when he'd died, five years earlier. Since his death, he'd been lingering as a spirit on earth, watching Carol Sullivan live the same life he'd had—making the same heartless, callous mistakes.

"Well, I'm partly to blame." Tony had never been kind to Carol. As a result of that—and other contributing factors from her past—she'd grown to become as cold and lonely as an iceberg, and drifting into an ever-melting, lifeless existence just the same.

"She can't even hear or see me," Tony continued. "How am I supposed to save her?"

Some living people had a gift—the ability to see and hear ghosts. The so-called mediums, however, were few and far between—and Carol wasn't one of them.

"She doesn't have any friends or family who can see ghosts. Without an intermediary, I can't reach out to her." Tony had been reduced to helplessly watching Carol ruin her life.

Burke pulled the cigarette out of his mouth and flicked nonexistent ashes off the glowing orange tip. He stared at one wall of the pawnshop—where yellow paint was peeling from the plaster. Tony kept quiet. He recognized Burke's narrow-eyed gaze of contemplation.

Tony hadn't known Burke in life. He'd never have

associated with a pawnshop owner. In death, however, Burke had become his best friend. Tony wished he'd taken time to make friendships like this while he'd still been alive—but being a ghost was all about languishing in regret, wasn't it?

Burke scratched at his large belly.

"Save her, eh? Might be a way to—but not in the way you think."

"I'll try anything." Tony couldn't stomach the thought of a talented young surgeon like Carol dying before she recognized the opportunity to turn her life around.

"You can make your case to the Christmas Spirits."

"The Christmas Spirits? They really exist?"

"Of course. Some spirits can be seen by whomever they choose at certain times of the year. The Christmas trio is already *real* busy this time of year, though. They're probably booked up. Some people start booking them a year in advance."

"They could help me help Carol?"

"They don't save lives. They save souls."

Tony's posture slumped. He wanted both for Carol— her life and her soul—and Christmas was only a week away. What were the chances his Christmas miracle could be worked into the busy schedules of the Christmas Spirits?

But he had to try—for Carol.

"So, is it like in the stories?" Tony asked. "The Christmas Spirits can save a soul in one night?" He sighed as he considered this. "They'd have to. She wouldn't have very long to live after that." He pressed the palms of his hands into his eyes, trying to block out the future image he'd seen of Carol getting hit by a truck on Christmas morning.

In his vision, she'd distractedly walked to the curb.

She'd stepped over the edge.

The end.

Burke shrugged, though his eyes looked at Tony with compassion.

"At least she'd have salvation. She can set things in motion to give her peace as a spirit. She wouldn't be lingering, like you—stuck wondering how to fix the cold-hearted deeds of her life."

"Okay. I'll do it. Where can I find the Christmas Spirits?"

"This close to Christmas? They oughta be at Michigan Avenue, under the Chicago Christmas tree."

CHAPTER 2

Carol Sullivan carried a coffee in one hand and her phone in the other as she walked to the surgical intensive care unit. Her heels clicked on the linoleum floor, and her white coat gleamed beneath the fluorescent lights.

On her phone, she checked her email and her schedule. She had an OR case at 10 a.m. and maybe an hour break before two more surgeries. When Carol reached the work station, her physician assistant, John Baker, stood abruptly from where he'd been sitting.

He banged his knee against the countertop in his haste, and rubbed it as he stammered: "Good morning, Dr. Sullivan."

Carol Sullivan appraised Johnny's white coat—which was actually stained a dingy yellow and had frayed elbows. His shoes were the same scuffed, worn Burkenstocks she'd been staring at for years. She'd repeatedly told him to buy new apparel—so he could appear more professional—but he'd ignored her request each and every time.

"What's the status?" Carol snapped.

Johnny handed her a single sheet of paper containing her patient list. "Mr. Smith is recovering nicely. We'll be pulling his chest tube today." Johnny glanced up at her briefly. "The patient was wondering if you'd stop by to see him today. He's day three post-op, and he said he hasn't seen you since his surgery."

Carol blinked irritably. "Johnny, do you know how much insurance pays for an inpatient post-op follow-up visit by a surgeon? Zero. Nada. Nothing. Zilch. That's why I have you. I do the surgeries; you see the patients while they're in the hospital. I get paid for one outpatient clinic follow-up visit—that's it."

Disappointment seemed to ooze from the visible pores on Johnny's broad forehead and generously sized nose.

"I don't make the rules," Carol added with a shrug.

Johnny pushed his glasses up on his nose and continued: "Mr. Johnson's family is asking what the next steps are. He's post-op day twenty-six. He's the one with…"

"…post-op pneumonia. Yes, I know. The plan is; he *can't* recover from his pneumonia—his lungs aren't strong enough. I warned him and his family that resecting his lung cancer was high risk."

"Oh, they understand that. They're not upset about his care—but they think he wouldn't want to be on life support the way he is now."

Carol's left eye twitched. "They want to pull life support?"

"Yes. If he's not going to survive, they want to stop it."

"Well, they can't. Not until he's post-op day thirty-one. Five days."

"But…"

"Stop gaping at me. You know how damaging thirty-day post-op mortality is to a surgeon and the hospital. Half the thoracic surgeons in the country would've turned down Mr. Johnson's case, but I chose to try to help him. My reward is to have his death increase my thirty-day mortality statistics? I don't think so. Again, I didn't make this rule, and all it does is damage those of us who are willing to be more aggressive. Other surgeons cherry-pick the healthiest cases."

Johnny hesitated. "But he's a patient, not a number."

"If only the national benchmarks we're judged by took that into account," Carol snapped back.

"What do you want me to tell the patient?"

"It's Christmas Eve. They don't want him to die on Christmas. Keep him alive until after Christmas and everyone's had a chance to enjoy the holidays."

Johnny nodded, but looked unconvinced.

Carol sipped her coffee before prompting the physician assistant. "Next patient?"

"The radiation oncologist wants to start Mr. Brown on radiation therapy, but we need to control his atrial fibrillation first."

"Good. Get him moved out of my ICU."

Johnny blinked at her.

Carol pursed her lips. "He's stage four. I can't fix him. I've taken care of his pleural effusion. Now, the intensivists can fix his atrial fibrillation."

"I know—it's just hard on patients to change teams."

"We've got three patients who are going to be post-op by the end of the day. I need those beds open." As if reading Johnny's expression, Carol admitted: "Yes, there's an assembly line to surgery—and, yes, it's impersonal. However, warm and fuzzy doesn't pay anyone's bills."

"Yes, ma'am."

Carol took a deep breath to rein in her frustration. She felt like she shouldn't have to justify all of her actions to her physician assistant. Johnny knew how things functioned on the surgical service. Were his gushing emotions a direct result of the holiday season? Why did people get so sentimental during the period of a commercialized, staged event like Christmas?

Carol glanced at her watch. "I need to scrub in."

"Oh, and your office assistant called," Johnny added. "She said Mr. Forte is asking when he can schedule his lung volume reduction surgery."

Carol raised her hands in the air—phone in one, coffee in the other—indicating the situation was out of her control. "His insurance company won't approve it. If I do the procedure, I'm strapping him with a hefty bill for an elective procedure."

"His breathing is getting worse."

"Of course it is. His upper lobes are like Swiss cheese from emphysema."

"You could appeal the case."

"Did you know that insured people have more medical debt than the uninsured? That is how bad our medical care has gotten. It's unfathomable. People can't even afford deductibles—*deductibles*." She shook her head and left, stalking off toward the OR.

✳

CAROL FINISHED HER PRE-OPERATIVE DOCUMENTATION. While waiting for the OR to open itself to her cases, she walked back to her office in the surgical services building.

"Carol!"

She stiffened—startled at the chipper voice. Then, with a scowl, she turned around.

"Hello, Mel."

Without invitation, Carol's younger sister wrapped her arms around the surgeon and squeezed. Melanie was always cheerful, and Carol suspected pediatricians were all secretly dosed with antidepressants to maintain this state of perpetual happiness. How else could they be able to be all smiles around snot-nosed children, when their reimbursement rates were no better than those of a family doctor, or even a physician assistant?

Mel beamed a smile. "Did you get my text? Are you coming to our Christmas Eve party?"

Carol gestured at her scrubs. "Surgeries."

Melanie's smile remained undeterred. She wore a red knit cap with short curls protruding from beneath the edges. Her sweater was covered with tiny reindeer, set against a backdrop of green and red stripes.

"You should come by when you're done. Pike and I'll be up late celebrating."

Carol fought not to roll her eyes.

Celebrating? That meant gift-giving, junk food-eating, and excessive drinking—all the commercialized pursuits merchants wanted people to indulge in during the

Christmas period. Spend. Spend. Spend. Meanwhile, credit card debt across the country soared.

Melanie shook her head. "All work and no play."

Carol pursed her lips. "The need for surgeries doesn't take a break just because the rest of the country does."

Melanie gave Carol a look of pity, even as she maintained her dimpled smile.

"Except it doesn't always have to be *you* doing the surgery, Carol—*every* holiday, *every* year."

Before Carol could protest, Melanie kissed her sister's cheek and bounded away down the hall, back toward the elevator.

Carol finished her final surgery for the day—a thoracic aortic aneurysm repair—and returned to the physician locker room. It was only four in the afternoon, but most people had already left early since it was Christmas Eve. Apparently, most other people were like her sister Melanie—and wanted to spend the holidays with their families.

Carol didn't share that same sentimentality. Her life was entirely career oriented. She'd chosen between her career and a relationship—and while she felt she shouldn't have *had* to choose, she hadn't worked relentlessly every day and gotten into one of the best surgical residencies in the country, just to give it all up for a man.

Even if he'd been *the man*—the one for her in a way she knew she'd never have again.

So, why bother after that? Carol hadn't. She hadn't dated since Liam left.

She changed out of her scrubs and back into her skirt suit. When she closed her locker, the lights above flickered.

Odd.

The metal doors of the lockers rattled on their hinges.

Carol backed away from them. Was this an earthquake? Here in Chicago? Except, the rest of the room wasn't shaking; only the lockers shimmied.

She felt her heart race. Was she hallucinating? She *had* drunk three cups of coffee today, on a still-empty stomach.

Suddenly, a man emerged from one end of the room.

Carol gasped. In a hoarse voice, she croaked: "This is the women's locker room!"

"Hello, Carol. You look well."

Carol squinted her eyes. "Tony?"

She blinked. "Tony… You—you can't be here."

Carol knew Tony—or *had* known Tony. They'd worked together. He'd died about five years earlier from a heart attack. Carol had even gone to his funeral.

Well, she'd sent flowers—or, maybe it was a wreath.

It didn't matter. She'd had too many cases. She couldn't have cancelled them all for the funeral of a coworker.

The figure of Carol's long-deceased thoracic surgery partner took a step forward.

"It's me, Carol—I'm here. But only for tonight, just this once." Tony walked closer.

He appeared to Carol just as she remembered him—

in his seventies, with a full head of gray hair. However, he looked pale. No, more than pale. More than *deathly* pale.

In fact, he looked downright transparent.

"This isn't possible," Carol stammered, taking a step back from him.

"It *is* possible." Tony raised his hands reassuringly. "When you make your life only about you, *this* is possible." He gestured to his ghostly body—because Carol could now see that her former coworker *was* a ghost. "It's possible to be doomed to a spirit existence—a curse for my selfishness."

Carol shook her head, stepping nervously backwards from his shimmering, translucent figure. "W-what do you mean, selfish? You saved lives, Tony! You performed the most surgeries of any thoracic surgeon in the state."

While Carol could hardly claim to have been close to Dr. Tony Olsen, she wouldn't hesitate to admit that he'd been the best thoracic surgeon she'd ever trained under and worked with.

"Oh, I saved lives—just like you," he nodded. "Sure. I performed surgeries—but that was my *job*; and I performed my job with cold detachment. Those were people I was fixing—not cars."

"You can't get attached, Tony—you taught me that. You told me if you showed even the slightest hint of compassion, the medical system would suck the life out of you."

"I was wrong, Carol—*dead* wrong." Tony shrugged. "Now, I'm just dead."

"What *are* you?" Carol's analytical mind was at work. A

ghost? Specter? Wraith? What were the differences between them?

"I'm a spirit who can't move on. Don't become like me, Carol."

Carol's temper suddenly flared white hot. "Since when did you give a damn about *me*?"

"Since I died," Tony admitted. "Since I realized I trained you wrong. I emphasized the surgery, not the patient." He paused and then added, "And you're right to be angry—I was just as rotten to you as I was to my patients. I had you work too many long hours. Liam left you because I worked you too hard—just like my wife left me."

Carol stood there, shaking. She hadn't realized Tony had known about Liam. She stiffened. It wasn't any of Tony's business. She wrapped her arms around her waist.

"I haven't eaten today," the surgeon said to herself. "That's all this is." Medically, she knew prolonged fasting could cause delirium. She needed to eat and hydrate, and then she'd stop seeing visions of her old mentor.

The lockers rattled again, and then the room seemed to close in all around her. Carol shrank back, tightening her arms around herself.

"Change, Carol!" Tony warned. "Don't become a lost spirit." He paused, raising a ghostly finger. "Tonight, you'll be visited by three ghosts."

"What? *No.*" Despite her terror, Carol's cynicism rose to the forefront. "This is ludicrous."

"Three..." Tony began in a booming voice.

"...let me guess," Carol interrupted him. "The first one at 1 a.m.?"

Tony blinked. "Yes. How did you know that?"

Carol pinched the bridge of her nose. "No. Stop it, Tony. Whatever this is, you need to make it stop."

"Three ghosts!" Her deceased coworker warned, his voice growing supernaturally deep.

Suddenly, the lockers loomed closer over Carol, and terror overwhelmed her. She began to hyperventilate. Grated metal surrounded her—smothered her—until Carol closed her eyes and screamed in terror.

And then—nothing happened.

Moments later, when Carol dared to open her eyes again, she found the locker room restored to its usual condition—upright and immobile, with a bench in between each row of lockers.

CHAPTER 3

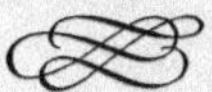

Carol hurried out of the hospital, intending to go directly home and have a large glass of Scotch. She stomped down the street, hands in the pockets of her thick coat, and scarf flapping behind her in the breeze.

Yet, Carol didn't feel the biting cold. She didn't feel anything.

She plowed past Christmas trees, carolers, and stores decorated in green, red, and gold. She felt the joy in none of it. It was all sentimental commercialism designed to get people to overspend money they didn't have.

During residency, Carol had been forced to work the holidays. During surgery fellowship, she was the one without a spouse or children, so she'd always been coerced into covering the holiday schedule. Finally, when Carol had earned the clout to make someone *else* work Christmas, she figured—why bother?

Let the rest of them have their celebration and waste their money.

Carol paused at the corner. She had the choice of

several paths home, but she always opted for the same one, which took her past the art gallery. She often stopped there during her lunch breaks, or on her way home.

Carol crossed the street. She'd only been intending to walk past it, but was instead surprised to find The Stardust Gallery still open on Christmas Eve.

She walked inside, and the scent of cinnamon wafted toward her with the warm air.

Carol took a familiar path directly to her favorite painting. It was of three horses—black, white, and brown—running through the frothy surf on a beach. Behind them, the setting sun lit the sky in vibrant orange. Something about the image of the glistening beach, wide ocean, and expansive horizon captured a sense of freedom. The horses were free to run—free from riders, free from the confines of a fence, and free from obligation.

Carol looked down at the signature in the bottom left corner: *L Charron.*

"Do you like it?" A man's voice sounded in her ear.

"I love it." Carol surprised herself with that confession. She turned to look at the man who'd asked her, standing beside her on the gallery floor.

"Liam?" Her eyes widened. "Oh, my gosh! *Liam!*"

Without even thinking about it, Carol reached out and embraced the artist. In the few seconds the hug lasted, the last conversation they'd had flooded into her mind.

Stiffening, Carol stepped back, regaining her composure and straightening her scarf.

She was angry with herself. She'd had no right to hug Liam. That scare in the locker room must have affected her judgment.

"How are you, Carol?"

Liam grinned. He looked magnificent, wearing a sleekly tailored tuxedo. He was clean-shaven, and his wavy dark hair was brushed neatly back.

Carol stared at him. Had it really been five years? Liam looked every bit as good as the day he'd left her. His voice was the same soothing baritone.

"I'm good." Carol cleared her throat. "Really good."

She turned back to the painting. "Your work has always been breathtaking, Liam."

"Thank you." He chuckled softly. "I'm glad you like it. We're having a silent auction—a fund-raiser for the children's hospital."

Carol shook her head with a smile. Liam always gave so much of his hard work to charity. She remembered the many hours he'd spend painting and picking colors. He agonized over every brushstroke—but in the end, his creations always seemed magical.

"Since you like it so much," Liam added, "it would be remiss of me not to mention that it's for sale."

Carol said nothing.

Most days, she always found time to stop by The Stardust Gallery to see this particular painting. She'd never seen Liam here before, though. He didn't involve himself in the direct sale of his own work—except, of course, for fundraisers.

Carol stared at the painting. She'd grown so accustomed to seeing Liam's art, to having this small piece of him so close to where she worked, that the thought someone else might buy it annoyed her. She already considered the painting hers.

"The colors are so vibrant," Carol said, staring at the painting. "The brushstrokes capture the powerful muscles of the horses."

But she couldn't buy it. It was impractical. The colors matched nothing in her home, and she didn't have room for the enormity of it, in any case.

Liam had once told her he sought to create masterpieces that people would design a room around, rather than vice versa.

This was such a painting. A masterpiece.

"Did you ever start riding again?" Liam asked.

Still staring at the painting, Carol answered: "No."

She hadn't ridden horses since medical school. It had been a brief passion and a hobby of hers once, made possible by a friend who had let her ride his horses at no cost to her. But the eighty-hour work weeks during residency left no room for passions or hobbies.

Carol stood there stiffly. Although she was so close to Liam, standing with their shoulders nearly touching, she still felt like a great canyon divided them; a gorge filled with memories, regrets, and heartache.

She glanced down at his left hand. There was no ring, but that didn't mean he was single. Even if he was, it certainly did nothing to bridge the gaping divide between them.

A stocky, balding man came and stood on the other side of her and appraised the painting.

"It's *not* for sale," Carol snapped.

The man turned and looked up at her, eyes wide. Then, nervously, he moved to the next painting.

"Are you intending to buy it?" Liam asked with an amused tone.

"No." She paused. "I don't know. *He* can't have it."

Liam shook his head, expressing the disappointment she knew all too well. He stuck his hands into his pant pockets.

"Same old Carol. You can't bring yourself to indulge in the beauty and enjoyment of life."

Carol opened her mouth to criticize Liam, but his soft, sad eyes stole the fight from her. Instead, she felt the corners of her lips curl.

"Same old Liam—always trying to revive love in the world, one masterpiece at a time."

He gave her a smile that had Carol instantly wanting to crawl back into his arms.

Instead, she pulled her coat tighter around her and snapped: "I should go." She paused, before adding: "I hope your auction does well."

"It was wonderful to see you again, Carol."

A lump formed in the back of her throat. "Goodbye, Liam."

A moment later, she stumbled back out onto the street —where it was the cold that stung her eyes. She stomped down the sidewalk, arms wrapped around herself.

How could her emotions for Liam still be so strong after five years?

How could he stand there and talk so civilly after everything that had happened?

He left me, she reminded herself.

Carol walked fast toward home, plowing through

carolers and avoiding eye contact with all the people peddling for donations.

She wasn't hungry, but she stopped and ordered dumplings and egg-drop soup from a Chinese takeout restaurant one block from her brownstone anyway.

Once she finally arrived home, Carol traded her skirt for cotton pajama bottoms and ate in the quiet stillness of her home in front of her computer.

While she ate, she reviewed labs and chest x-rays through the electronic healthcare record system. Then, she tossed her trash and moved from her couch to her bed, where she reviewed a few medical journals in her field followed by a final breeze through her email.

When Carol couldn't keep her eyes open any longer, she drifted into a deep sleep.

CAROL WOKE to the darkness of her bedroom and a scratching noise against one widow.

She turned her head and focused her eyes—and saw a clawed, gnarled hand scraping along the outside of her window.

Carol was instantly awake. She bolted upright and blinked in terror, but it wasn't a hand scraping the window—it was just a bare, black branch with the moonlit sky serving as a backdrop. The wind had caused the tentacle-like twigs of the branch to scrape against her window.

Heart still pounding, Carol reached for her phone as she tossed the blanket off.

1 a.m.

A shuffling noise suddenly emerged from her living room, and Carol's heart started pounding again. She sucked in a breath, quietly slipping out of bed and pulling her robe around her.

The shuffling noise continued. This wasn't her imagination—someone was out there!

Should she turn the light on? Wouldn't that make her as visible to her attacker as her attacker would be to her?

Carol looked around desperately for a weapon, but found only a shoe. She picked it up anyway, brandishing it like a weapon with the point of the heel facing out.

With the shoe extended in her trembling hand, Carol tiptoed out of her bedroom, down the hallway, and into the living room.

By the light of a gentle moon, she saw no dangerous figures standing in the darkness.

Heart still pounding, she scanned the shadows—but nothing threatening emerged.

Damn, Tony.

He'd gotten her worked up for nothing.

Distant music suddenly sounded. Carol turned, watching as the edges of her front door became framed in bright white light.

Was this a prank?

She trod closer to the door, trying to listen over the sound of her pounding heart. What was that music? *Silent Night?*

Was it carolers? Out this late?

Carol wrenched the front door open, ready to scold whoever was waking her up in the middle of the night, only to find a small child standing on her doorstep—a child of perhaps seven or eight.

The chorus of singing dwindled to a stop. Carol stood there and looked down. A glowing halo of light was surrounding the curly red hair of the little girl on Carol's doorstep.

The little girl looked angelic and had Carol gaping in awe…

…until stark terror suddenly struck her.

Three ghosts!

She wrenched her silk robe tighter around her, and in a breathless whisper demanded: "Are you the first?"

The little girl nodded softly. "I'm the Ghost of Christmas Past." Her voice was gentle and high-pitched.

Carol sucked in a breath.

"Well, what if I don't want to see the past?"

"Surely, you wouldn't close the door to your own chance at redemption, would you?"

"Redemption," Carol scoffed. "I help people every day. You're telling me that's not enough?"

"You do your job, and people are helped because of it—but you do what benefits you and your financial status. Your job is noble, but your tactics are not. Your intentions have become tainted."

Carol narrowed her eyes at the spirit. She might *look* like a child—with her red plaid skirt, black tights, and pine-green sweater—but she didn't *talk* like one.

Carol tied off her robe with a huff. "Okay. Let's get this over with, then."

The Ghost of Christmas Past extended her arm, and Carol dropped the shoe she'd forgotten she'd been holding. She took the small child's hand, pulling the door of her brownstone closed behind her.

Something that felt like a frightening leap of faith engulfed Carol. All around them, the Christmas decorations on the other brownstones glowed brighter and brighter, before finally blurring into great smears of green, red, and white.

Carol blinked several times, and when her vision cleared, she found herself outside a row of small townhouses. They were decorated with meager strings of Christmas lights, and the buildings looked faded and dingy. Small yards were closed in with chain-link fences.

A dark-haired girl was being dropped off by a school bus, and she lugged her backpack over to one of the townhouse doors. After pulling a key from around her neck, she unlocked the door and let herself inside.

The Ghost of Christmas Past followed the little girl, and Carol followed the ghost—in through the front door of her childhood home. This was a place she'd almost forgotten. It looked even more desolate than she'd remembered it.

Inside, all the rooms were tiny. Even the kitchen was so small that nobody could get access the refrigerator if someone else was cooking at the stove.

The walls were covered in peeling floral wallpaper— yellowed from time and stains. The smell of stale cigarettes hung in the air.

When the little girl crept quietly to her room, Carol and the ghost followed. Carol recalled how she'd had to be quiet whenever she came home from school, because her mother worked nights and didn't want Carol waking her up.

"You remember this place?" the ghost asked.

"I remember," Carol said flatly. "Mom worked nights. Dad worked days. They didn't see much of each other—or me."

The girl—Young Carol—flopped onto her bed in her tiny bedroom and opened a Nancy Drew book.

"You liked to read books," the ghost said. "You liked fiction."

"I liked escaping every afternoon into a book," Carol retorted. "I could enter a world in which I wasn't an unwanted child, a nuisance, and another mouth to feed."

Perhaps that was harsh. Carol's parents had always kept her and her sister fed, in school, and in a safe environment. They'd provided adequately for them—but Carol couldn't ever remember feeling truly cherished.

She watched her younger self turn the page of her book.

"It was in one of those adventures that I decided to pursue medicine." The ghost looked up at Carol, her red curls swaying from the motion. "*Nancy Drew. Case File number 35, Bad Medicine.*"

Carol chuckled. "That's right."

It was after reading that book that Carol had solidified how she'd wanted to help people—to better society. She'd planned to make a difference and be someone worthy of note—someone worthy of the affection of others.

Someone who was more than just an annoying kid with a key around their neck and an overactive imagination.

Carol did the math in her head. Her sister Melanie would still have been at daycare during the time of this memory. When Melanie was old enough for grade school, she became Carol's responsibility—a parent when they had no parents present. Carol had cooked for her and her sister and made sure Melanie did her homework.

When Carol had turned thirteen, her parents, who'd already lived practically separate lives beneath the same roof, finally divorced.

Despite her parent's unconcealed disinterest in each other, the separation had still been a shock to young Carol. Melanie, five years younger, had taken it hard as well, and Carol had felt she'd have to put on a front of toughness for Melanie's sake.

Carol had spent her teen years only seeing her father on occasional weekends and holidays—all of which she'd had to arrange herself, since her parents only spoke to each other through their respective lawyers.

After Carol had finally left for college, many years after this memory had taken place, she hadn't bothered coming back home except to see Melanie.

"What happened to that child? The one who dreamed of making the world a better place?" The ghost blinked up at Carol.

"Reality," Carol replied, coldly.

CHAPTER 4

The house aged before Carol's eyes—the wallpaper peeling further and becoming a dingier yellow while the furniture shifted and changed as it was replaced over the years. She then found herself watching a twenty-year-old version of herself sneak into the house, carrying two glasses of eggnog and a gold, foil-wrapped present under her arm.

With the stealth of a mouse, twenty-year-old-Carol had slipped into Melanie's room.

Carol had been away at college at the time of this memory; but remembered returning on this occasion to spend the holiday with her family—or rather Melanie, since their mother was working.

"Carol!"

"Shhh. Merry Christmas." Carol handed Melanie a glass of eggnog and the wrapped gift. "It's after midnight, so I thought we'd celebrate together now."

"Why didn't you give this to me earlier tonight? When

we did family gift exchange?" Melanie hugged her sister. "Besides, you already gave me a gift."

Young Carol took a sip of eggnog as she sat beside Melanie on the on the bed.

"Those were cheap decoy earrings," she explained. "This is the *real* gift. I can't give it to you in front of Mom. You know how she gets all huffy when we spend too much money on frivolous things."

"Oh? Something frivolous?" Melanie held the box next to hear ear and shook it with eager anticipation. Then, she dropped it into her lap before tearing off the paper with the ferocity of a groundhog clawing through dirt.

When she opened the gift, Melanie gasped. "It's the dress!"

She leapt out of bed and held the gown against her body. "Mom said I couldn't have it!"

"Well, Mom didn't buy it."

"But it was expensive!"

"Shhh." Carol shrugged. "I've been tutoring organic chemistry. Besides, you look gorgeous in it, and I know you want to go to prom."

Present-day Carol hugged herself as she watched the memory replay in front of her. "She did look beautiful that night."

"You doted on her like your mother never doted on you," the ghost responded.

"I sure did." Carol sighed. "Probably spoiled her rotten."

Except Carol knew Melanie was anything but rotten, and she'd gone on to become a pediatrician adored by both children and their parents. Carol was so proud of her.

But Melanie gave too much of herself. People took advantage—both of her time and her money. Melanie would never retire the way she earned so little and spent so much—mostly on other people. Her sister's husband—a graphic designer—wasn't any more frugal than Melanie, but his heart was just as big and sappy as hers.

THEN, the room twisted and contorted around them again, until it finally morphed into a completely different location. This was an office—the walls decorated with numerous bookshelves, all stuffed with medical text-books. Diplomas and plaques hung from the walls.

This was no Christmas memory.

Carol saw herself at the age of twenty-four—with her long hair flowing down her back. She was sitting in the office across from a stony-faced man behind a desk.

Carol's stomach clenched. She remembered this man —this surgeon—all too well. He'd been in charge of the medical student surgical rotation, and he'd had the cruelest reputation for pimping students and belittling them on rounds. Surviving his wrath had been like surviving a hazing.

"Dr. Sullivan," the stony-faced man began, looking down at twenty-four-year-old Carol over his long, curved nose, "you don't want to be a surgeon."

"I do, sir," Carol replied. "I'm here to ask you for a letter of recommendation for my ERAS, because that's exactly what I want to be."

Carol was applying for residency, and she needed a letter from a surgeon endorsing her qualifications for a surgical specialty.

"Women sometimes *think* they want to specialize in surgery," the doctor's tone was cooly patronizing, "but they truly don't."

"They don't?"

"A four-week surgical rotation in medical school doesn't open your eyes to the demands of a surgeon. There are no work hour restrictions in the *real* world. Women pick surgery—and then they'll either change courses, or back out completely when they decide it's too difficult or they want a family."

A family? What business was it of this man if Carol wanted a family? She didn't even know if *she* wanted one. How could *he* know?

But the man continued: "It's a waste to fill a surgical residency spot with a woman who won't have the commitment to complete it, or the fortitude to become a dedicated surgeon."

Carol watched the eyes of her younger self grow wider, and her cheeks flush. She recalled being absolutely speechless at this humiliating encounter—a clear demonstration of sexual discrimination.

This man had known nothing of Carol's fortitude or dedication, but he had decided neither were sufficient based on her gender alone.

Present-day Carol paced the room and crossed her arms as the past version of herself sat in silent shock.

"Arrogant prick," Carol hissed. *"Save the spots for the men. They're better for the job."* She sneered angrily: "How many women did this monster turn away from surgical residencies with this speech?"

The old surgeon folded his hands on his desk. "Why don't you take some time to think it over? You could consider pediatrics—or, with your excellent grades, you could go to a dermatology residency."

"I wished I'd had the courage to give that jerk a piece of my mind," Carol said, watching her twenty-four-year-old-self squirm in the chair.

"But you didn't," the Ghost of Christmas Past reminded her, "and he did write you that letter."

"Damn right he did." Carol blew out a huff of air.

"You showed him," the little red-headed ghost added.

"Yes, I did."

"You became the dedicated, ruthless surgeon working long hours and forsaking a family that he didn't think you capable of."

Carol shot the ghost a sharp look. Before she could reply, the stuffy office—three-sizes too small for the surgeon's ego—collapsed in on itself.

A NEW ROOM coalesced around them—a workroom.

Carol instantly recognized the room, with computer stations lining two walls and a couch against another. In the middle of the room sat three rectangular plastic tables, each connected end-to-end to form a single, long table. This had been the workroom for surgical residents, and the night Carol and the Ghost of Christmas Past were visiting was Christmas Eve, some ten years earlier.

The tables were covered in plastic tablecloths, printed

with bright poinsettias. Food was spread across the table, a mixture of essential Christmas nutrition, like ham, sweet potatoes, deviled eggs, bread rolls, baked mac n' cheese, stuffing, turkey, and more—all brought in by the residents and their spouses. A half-dozen or so surgical residents were in the room, some working on computers and others playing computer games.

A younger Carol entered the room, wearing scrubs and looking worn. Her face brightened at the sight of the Christmas colors and the array of food. She walked to one end of the table and started making herself up a plate.

Clay was sitting in the workroom, too, with one foot propped up, stretching between the couch and the table and blocking young Carol's path. She scowled at her male counterpart. He was a tall, broad-shouldered blond man. Looking around the room, Carol noticed none of the other female surgeons were in the room. Clay always timed his harassment for when other women weren't around.

"Only those who brought food get to dine," Clay said.

"I brought food," Carol retorted.

"Oh, yeah. What?"

"The pecan pie." Carol stepped over his leg.

"That was yours? Wasn't bad. It's store-bought though —the other girls brought homemade dishes."

Carol refrained from reminding Clay that his female colleagues were *women*, not girls. She looked at the table, noticing the even mixture of both store-bought and homemade dishes, so plenty of men must have brought store-bought food. With a sniff, she continued to prepare herself a plate of dinner.

"So," she asked, as she loaded her plate, "because we're *women*, we're supposed to cook?"

Clay shrugged, and the gesture looked kind of like a 'yes'.

Present-day Carol pursed her lips, watching her younger self shoulder the abuse.

"He always made jabs like that," she remembered.

"Makes for a negative working environment," the ghost noted in her soft, childish voice.

"Yes—and he stole cases. Our physician mentors loved Clay because he was charismatic—and *male*, like them."

"The male physicians weren't *all* like him."

Carol shook her head. "No, of course not. Clay was the exception, not the rule. I had many very good and genuinely caring coworkers."

"Still," the little girl considered, "it must have made working here feel more like a battleground."

"All the jabs—medical school, residency, and fellowship—were like death by a thousand paper cuts." Carol thought she'd formed a barrier around these toxic memories, but judging by her visceral reaction at watching her own past, she realized maybe she hadn't fully healed from these events.

Shouldn't she look back on the negativity of the past and realize how it had made her stronger? Shouldn't she reflect with quiet appreciation how these men had made her a better woman—and a better physician—because of their sexism?

Instead, Carol felt hollow.

. . .

THE ROOM HARDENED, transforming into a two-dimensional acrylic painting, before the textured brush-strokes cracked and burst, turning to fine, colored particles and blowing away to reveal a brand new scene beneath.

This time, it was of the Chicago cityscape bathed in the glow of streetlights beneath a navy night sky. Christmas decorations filled the shopfronts along the street, while exhaust fumes from the heavy traffic puffed into the cold air before being whisked away by the brutal Chicago breeze.

Carol looked around and spotted the memory she was here to witness, watching herself emerge from the same hospital she worked at now.

This memory was also from Christmas, perhaps one year after the last memory she'd witnessed. The younger version of Carol was shivering, pulling herself into a thick, woolen coat. She nestled her cream-colored hat over a head of long, dark hair and set off into the chill at a brisk pace.

Present-day Carol remembered this eventful night. She'd just finished a shift and was off for the rest of the night. Off for Christmas Eve—but back to work for Christmas night.

Young Carol walked past carolers and Christmas trees. Horse-drawn carriages, decorated with holly and blinking lights, jingled down the road carrying rosy-cheeked couples bundled together beneath blankets.

...and visions of sugarplums danced through their head.

Magic had been in the air this night—it was palpable.

Carol heard one of her favorite Christmas songs: *Baby, It's Cold Outside*. She turned to see the source of the music.

A man was standing on the street corner, painting the enormous Christmas tree at Millennium Park on a large canvas. He'd set himself up with an easel and palette, and the work he was producing was exquisite. The artist had caught every detail of the glowing lights, reminiscent of a Thomas Kinkade painting, but still distinctly different to the man who'd been described as the Painter of Light.

Younger Carol approached the artist.

"It looks beautiful," she said to the backside of the painter, "but I'm surprised your paint isn't frozen stiff." She looked at his palette.

The man turned around and smiled at her.

She'd expected the painter to be someone older, but the man appeared to be only a few years older than she'd been at the time.

"Thank you." The artist rattled his pockets. "I keep a few tubes of acrylic in here, to keep them from solidifying."

Carol shivered. "It's a little chilly to be painting outside, isn't it?"

The artist rinsed his brush. "Actually, this is the warmest Christmas Eve Chicago has had in a decade. I couldn't miss the opportunity."

He gestured toward her scrubs. "Are you coming from work? Or going there?"

"Done with work."

"That's a blessing."

Was it? Carol never really understood that phrase, and "done with work" only meant until the next shift.

"Well, your tree is fantastic. Stay warm." Carol turned to leave.

"It's almost done," the artist rushed to say. "Wouldn't you like to wait and see the finished product?"

"These scrubs are paper thin," she shivered. "I need to get warm."

"Here." The artist pulled hand warmers from his pockets and gave them to her. "Give me ten minutes to finish. If you do, I'll buy you a hot meal in a warm restaurant."

Carol opened her mouth, about to object to this presumptuous dinner invitation from a complete stranger...

...but then, he smiled.

"I'm Liam."

Oh, that smile.

Young or present-day version, it didn't matter—neither Carol had ever seen something so warm and welcoming as Liam's smile. It was, in a word, *Christmas.* His smile was a radiant, festive gift.

"Carol." She smiled in return.

As Liam resumed painting, Carol noticed his expensive shoes and the fine, leather case for his painting supplies. This was no poor street artist, yet he'd still chosen to paint outdoors, on this cold, Christmas Eve.

When Liam finished, he let Carol take a photo of him beside his masterpiece—a masterpiece which he instantly dismissed as merely mediocre.

She shook her head. So far, the man's only flaw was his perfectionism.

Together, they packed his belongings into the leather

luggage bag and secured the finished painting in a tote bag. Liam turned off the Christmas music playing on his phone and slid the device into his pocket. Then, he insisted they ride to a nearby restaurant in one of the horse-drawn carriages. Carol balked at the over-priced impracticality.

"I've never ridden in one," Liam retorted, "and it's Christmas Eve. Relax. It'll be fun."

Liam pulled her into one of the carriages. His rough textured hands were warm.

Carol then watched her younger self get carried away in the carriage, sharing a blanket with a stranger who'd smelled like cinnamon and nutmeg.

"We talked until the restaurant closed," Carol told the child ghost, standing there wistfully. "I shared everything with that man, and I'd never shared myself with anyone before."

No one before Liam, and no one since he'd left.

"You still love him," the ghost said matter-of-factly.

Carol sniffed and bundled her robe tighter around her body. She couldn't feel the frigid chill from the night of this memory, but she felt cold nonetheless.

CHAPTER 5

The buildings and storefronts, adorned with their Christmas lights, blurred into a hazy Monet watercolor—before finally washing away completely to reveal bright, white lights.

As Carol blinked at the offending harsh light, an operating room came into focus around her, towering white walls and a sterile glow surrounding them. Beams of light concentrated on the exposed abdomen of a patient in the middle of surgery.

Carol watched a version of herself—this one in full sterile attire of gown, gloves, cap, and mask—assist a robust, older surgeon with a colon resection.

Present-day Carol's brain worked out from when this memory originated. She was observing herself as a resident, not long after having met Liam. Young Carol was no longer a medical student who watched from a distance or held retractors. She was directly contributing to this operation, moving intestines and suctioning blood. When the surgery eventually finished, Carol would be allowed to suture the abdomen shut.

The particular surgeon she'd been operating alongside that night was harsh. His hands moved fast with the practice of many years. He barked orders at Carol, and if she didn't move fast enough, he'd 'inadvertently' poke her with a needle and then blame her for it.

Carol remembered that her first surgeries with this surgeon had landed her three needle sticks and a series of blood tests in the weeks that followed, all to make sure she hadn't contracted any diseases from the patients.

Every surgical resident—male and female—knew the hazard of working with this surgeon, but everyone was too afraid to report his behavior. In hindsight, Carol suspected that if a half-dozen surgical residents had banded together to report him, the medical center would have been forced to investigate. Maybe not, though, if the whistleblowers had all been women.

"I hated him." Carol seethed as her chill from earlier was replaced by heated anger.

Her blood boiled as she stood once again in the same OR as this egotistical, maniacal surgeon, watching her terrified younger self try to help, while avoiding injury.

Carol knew this painful trip down memory lane was supposed to be a lesson, so she pre-empted the Ghost of Christmas Past by clarifying: "I've never been, and never will be, anything like *him*."

How many times had this surgeon brought her to tears by making her feel inferior? Too slow. Too sloppy. How many times had he mumbled 'damn worthless surgeon' when they'd worked together?

Carol shook with rage at the memory of it.

"You're not like him," the ghost agreed. "Not yet."

The operating room faded to black.

A FAINT GLOW of green and red lit an entirely different room. A Christmas tree came into focus. Carol looked around and instantly recognized the room. It was the apartment she'd once shared with Liam.

The small apartment had a tiny gas fireplace, lit specially for the occasion, and the tree stood in one corner. Above the fireplace, the television was set to play Christmas music on repeat.

It wasn't Christmas, exactly, Carol recalled. She'd had to work December 23 through to December 27, so she and Liam were celebrating on December 28 instead.

Her younger self danced around the room wearing a low-cut, red velvet pajama set. Liam wore candy cane-covered flannel pajama pants—and nothing else.

"I love it! I love it!" Carol—Santa Carol, in those pajamas—exclaimed happily.

She gazed on the Christmas present Liam had given her—a stunning painting of human lungs with Liam's signature, artistic flare. He'd rendered the airway branches to look like the boughs of a tree, and the image was vividly life-like with blue and green leaves and breathtaking depth and shadow.

The timing of the gift had coincided with her acceptance into cardiothoracic surgery fellowship. Tears spilled down Carol's cheeks—both past-Carol and present-day

Carol. Liam took the Santa-adorned Carol into his arms and kissed her passionately.

He'd been so passionate.

His hands worked their way under her shirt as they kissed their way to the couch. She ran her hands along his bare chest as he laughed and tumbled on top of her.

"I love you, Liam."

Present-day Carol reached out a hand and covered the ghost child's eyes. The spirit might be centuries older than her ghostly appearance suggested, but she still didn't need to see what had happened next.

Eventually, Carol recalled, she and Liam had returned to gift giving, and Liam opened the new set of brushes she'd bought him.

Present-day Carol turned back to stare at Liam's painting of the lung-tree. She still had that painting to this day. She'd carefully wrapped it up and stored it in her closet, because it had become too painful to look at. The beautiful painting was a reminder of what she'd lost—what she'd let go.

OBJECTS SHIFTED and shimmered around them, and then the same apartment went fast-forward two years into the future.

Young Carol and Liam were arguing.

With a wave of nausea, present-day Carol remembered this fight—their last fight. Ever.

With raised voices, the two of them had bickered about a familiar topic: Carol was spending too much time at work, and Liam was feeling neglected.

"You're never home, Carol."

"I have a job, Liam."

"A job that means more to you than I do!"

Present-day Carol tuned out the painful exchange of words. Regardless of the excuses she'd made—career advancement, being better than the competition, and being needed by patients—enough time had passed since this last fight for her to reflect, ruminate, and accept the truth behind the excuses.

"I don't want to see this," Carol told the ghost beside her. "I've already been through the pain of it once."

Once—and a thousand more times, as she'd replayed this memory over the years. She'd replayed it so many times, it was redundant to watch it yet again.

The truth was that no one had ever loved her as completely as Liam had, and she'd never been able to bring herself to feel as though she deserved him.

Carol never felt worthy of his love.

"You're smothering me!" Young Carol was shouting at Liam.

Carol cringed at the sound of her own words. When she saw the crushed look on Liam's face, her heart felt like it was breaking all over again. She collapsed to her knees, clutching her stomach.

"Stop," she begged the little girl. "Please, make it stop. Why are you showing me this? I can't change the past."

"The past cannot be changed," the redhead replied, "but it doesn't have to be repeated."

"I don't want to repeat it. That's why I never went back to him."

"There's another way," the voice of the small ghost trailed off, and then she vanished.

CAROL WIPED away tears and looked up.

As she composed herself, she looked around. She was kneeling on the floor of her brownstone, surrounded by the familiar, soft gray walls. Her heart pounded with a dull ache.

In panicked haste, she reached for her phone and dialed Liam's number.

Did he even still have the same number?

The call went straight to voicemail.

"Liam, it's Carol," her words came out rushed. "I just..."

Her voice trailed off. What did she want? She just wanted to hear his voice, but that seemed like a ridiculous thing to say. Instead, Carol finished her message: "I just wanted to wish you a Merry Christmas. It was good to see you today."

Still on the line, Carol forced herself to take a deep breath. As she did so, she looked up and caught sight of the clock on the wall.

1:45 a.m.

She bit back a groan. How inappropriate to call Liam so late! Could she delete the voicemail? Possibly, but he'd still see that she'd called.

"...and don't sell the horse painting—*please*."

With that, Carol disconnected the call.

She tossed the phone aside and deflated back to the floor. She felt empty, like her insides had been scooped out, and the little girl had been just the first of her scheduled supernatural visitors.

How much time until the next ghost arrived to further emotionally torture her?

Carol had thought she'd effectively buried the past, but now the memories were back—fresh and raw after the Ghost of Christmas Past had forced her to revisit them.

The pain now felt days old, rather than dulled by the passing years. Carol had forgotten how much she'd distanced herself from these memories, and that wasn't the only thing.

She thought of Melanie. She'd distanced herself from her sister, too. They'd been so close once.

And Liam. Carol had forgotten how hard she'd pushed him away. He'd been so loving that she'd felt inadequate in her reciprocation, but instead of trying harder, her response had been to distance herself from him.

Could she ever be the compassionate older sister that Melanie deserved? Or the doting companion in a balanced relationship? Could Carol rediscover that side of herself? Or was that a gorge too far to cross?

She stumbled to the bathroom and splashed cold water on her face. Staring at herself in the mirror, Carol brushed the tangles out of her dark, shoulder-length hair. In her reflection, her brown eyes looked tired and her cheekbones pale.

She took a deep breath and stood up straight. Then, with determination, Carol strode into the bedroom and changed into blue jeans and a forest green sweater. She might not have any choice about being dragged around

Chicago by supernatural entities, but she didn't have to be wearing a silk robe as she did so.

When Carol walked into the kitchen to get herself a glass of water, she froze.

A burly, bald man in torn overalls and stained work boots was standing there.

Were it not for his green sweater—with Rudolf sporting a flashing red nose on it—Carol might have thought this new arrival was a burglar. The ghostly stranger grinned at her, and she relaxed somewhat. A shaggy beard encased his smile, but it was warm and genuine.

"I'm the Ghost of Christmas Present."

"You look more like a janitor," she responded coolly. "I'm Carol, your next victim."

The ghost gave a hearty laugh, one that seemed to reverberate throughout the room. The warmth of his mirth even spread through Carol, dispelling the cold clinging to her after watching her wretched past.

"Shall we begin?" The spirit's voice was a deep baritone.

"Lead the way," Carol answered, devoid of enthusiasm.

The Ghost of Christmas Present led Carol through a doorway, one that had materialized where her refrigerator had once been.

Carol found herself standing in a tiny apartment, decorated festively with a small tree and a string of lights stretched across the border between the walls and ceiling. A bald-headed boy sat in front of the tree, beneath which lay a solitary present.

Carol walked forward, confident that the hairless boy

couldn't see or hear her. She observed the paleness of his skin and the dark bruises on his arms.

"Cancer?"

"Unfortunately, yes," the Ghost of Christmas Present replied. "Leukemia."

"Whose son is he?"

"Corey, let's do this!" The answer came in the sound of a cheerful voice. Carol's physician assistant, Johnny, walked into the room wearing blue and white snowflake decorated cotton pajamas and black slippers.

Carol glanced at the shoes by the door to the apartment. They were the same, worn loafers she'd been annoyed at day after day—hanging beneath the familiar, elbow-shredded white coat of her physician assistant.

Johnny's wife entered the room, looking tired, but with a warm smile on her face at seeing her son by the tree. "Open it, Corey."

The boy tore into the present.

"Only one?" Carol asked.

The ghost didn't reply.

"An Xbox!" Corey's face lit with a smile. He stopped before opening the box. "But you said it would cost too much, because we needed to cover the cost of chemo."

Johnny rubbed the top of his head. "I got a bonus."

Carol choked at the lie. A lump of coal hit her stomach like a rock dropping into a well.

She didn't set Johnny's salary—that was done by the hospital—but she knew his wages were in the bottom third of the national average. Someone with his level of experience and dedication ought to make a lot more.

Carol glanced at the Ghost of Christmas Present.

"I can talk to administration—argue for a raise." Her voice was a dry whisper.

"You said it yourself," the ghost responded, "the insured have the highest amount of medical debt. Johnny earns enough that he simultaneously doesn't qualify for medical financial assistance, but also can't cover the large deductible and out-of-pocket expenses for his son's treatment."

Carol gulped dryly. "I'll talk to administration about getting him a bonus, too."

The ghost nodded, stroking his beard.

The boy's mother came back into the small living room and handed Corey a mug of hot chocolate.

"Thanks, Mom. Thanks for the gift! I'm going to set it up!"

As Corey went to the television, Johnny and his wife—Penny—moved to the kitchen. Carol tried to remember if she'd ever actually met Penny. No, she decided. She knew the name from Johnny mentioning her, but Penny had never come to see her husband at work, at least not while Carol had been around.

"You didn't get a bonus," Penny snapped at him.

"I know," Johnny nodded. "I just wanted to make him happy."

"Ugh." Penny groaned. "It's that horrible woman you work for. You need to find a better job."

Johnny kept his voice low. "We've been over this. Corey's best medical care is here in Chicago, and I can't work anywhere else in the city with my noncompete clause."

Penny lowered her head and stepped into his arms. "I

know. I'm sorry. Let's just make this the best Christmas we can for Corey."

Goosebumps prickled Carol's arms. Why the best? Had they been told this would be his last?

"Is Corey going to be okay?" Carol turned to the ghost, a pleading, shaky edge to her voice.

"I can't see the future," he replied dryly. "Only the present."

CHAPTER 6

The lights on Johnny's Christmas tree blurred, and a different living room, filled with a blue and white Christmas tree, slowly came into focus.

Melanie came into view, wearing the same festive colors from when Carol had seen her earlier, back when it had still been Christmas Eve. Carol stood in the living room of her younger sister's two-bedroomed loft.

The live Christmas tree was so plush that it filled one entire corner of the room and stretched so tall that the silver star brushed against the ceiling. Stockings hung over the gas-lit fireplace—four in all, each made from soft green and red velvet material. *Oh, Holy Night* played through a speaker system, while the couch was covered with Christmas pillows in vibrant gold and silver. Charles Dickens's *A Christmas Carol* sat in hardback on the mahogany coffee table.

As she stood there, Carol's sister held a framed photo, her expression uncharacteristically doleful. Melanie's husband, Pike, came into the room wearing red and green flannel pajamas. He towered over Melanie's small frame and wrapped gentle arms around her waist from behind.

Pike looked over Melanie's shoulder.

"The party was great. I'm sorry your sister didn't show."

"It was great." Melanie sighed. "I was hoping to give Carol her gift."

Carol peered closer at the framed photo in Melanie's hands.

A Christmas long ago was captured beneath the glass. In the picture, Carol was sixteen and had one arm slung over an eleven-year-old Melanie. They both wore Santa hats and broad smiles.

Carol swallowed and stepped back, watching Melanie gingerly tuck the photo in a decorative box and cushion it in white tissue paper.

"I wanted to tell her about..." Melanie's voice trailed off, and her hand lowered to her abdomen.

Carol looked back at the four stockings over the fireplace—one for Melanie, one for Pike, and one each for...

"Oh, Mel!" Carol's heart swelled with excitement for her little sister's expanding family. "She's pregnant!"

When Carol looked to the ghost for confirmation, he nodded.

"Twins?"

He laughed heartily. "Yes. Fortune has fallen upon them double-fold."

Carol smiled. "Thank you for showing me this, Spirit. I want to be a part of their lives. I want to be the best aunt they'll ever have."

"You'll be the *only* aunt they'll ever have." His eyes twinkled.

She nudged him with her elbow playfully, surprised that she could physically touch this supernatural entity. "You know what I mean."

With a swell of excitement, Carol looked back at her sister.

A BEEPING OF MACHINES SOUNDED, intruding on Carol's pleasant thoughts. Around her and the Ghost of Christmas Present, Melanie's apartment faded, replaced by a sterile ICU room. The beeping came from a monitor by a patient's bed, which showing a steady heartbeat and stable blood pressure. The ventilator supplied timed, incremental breaths through a breathing tube.

"Mr. Johnson." Carol let out an anguished sigh.

She looked at the ghost, whose bald head seemed to reflect the bright, fluorescent lights of the ICU room.

"I did what I could," Carol told him. "I tried to help him. He tolerated the surgery, but his lungs were too weak to come off the ventilator. Then, he contracted pneumonia."

The Ghost of Christmas Present dipped his head. "And his crime of failing to recover should doom him to being on life support? Which delays his inevitable death?"

"He isn't in pain," she replied. Mr. Johnson was comfortable on intravenous sedatives.

The large ghost motioned toward two women in the room, who sat in chairs watching over their loved one. Their drooping eyes and anguished expressions spoke volumes—a visual demonstration as to the extent of their suffering.

Carol raked her fingernails through her hair. "It's not my fault. Surgeons are graded based on their thirty-day mortality rate. If I pull the plug, I'm affecting my numbers —which, in the future, will only hurt other patients who..."

She stopped when she heard the quiet sobs of Mr. Johnson's wife.

Carol paced the room. "Okay, okay, I get it. These are people, not numbers. You've made your point, Spirit. Can we go now?"

The ghost hooked his thumbs through the straps of his overalls. The ICU room shimmered before transforming into a two-dimensional, vividly textured acrylic painting. The painting turned from the gloomy scene of a patient in a hospital bed to that of a beach at sunset.

The palm trees in the painting appeared so life-like that a real breeze might have made the painted leaves move.

Carol didn't have to look at the artist's name to know whose work this was.

Liam.

She knew those brush strokes. She knew the hands that had crafted this masterpiece.

As Carol watched, she saw Liam standing there— beside an elderly man who leaned on a cane. They both wore tuxedos, and Carol recognized the room as part of the gallery she'd visited on Christmas Eve. Side by side, the two men stared at the shimmering water of the painting.

"Have you ever loved something you couldn't have?" The old man asked that of Liam without turning his gaze from the textured rendition of water.

"Indeed I have, Mr. Moretti."

"Sometimes, the pain of it feels like a trickling bleed," the old man mused. "An ache that slowly, subtly takes your life."

"You're not wrong, sir." Liam moved to clasp his hands behind his back. "This will be my last auction, Mr. Moretti."

Shock registered on Mr. Moretti's face. "But you've done so well, Liam! The fund raiser has been stupendous, year after year."

"My heart isn't in it anymore. I apologize."

"What will you do?"

"Perhaps I need time. Perhaps I need to find a way to stop the hemorrhaging."

"Oh, Liam." Carol wanted to reach for him—to comfort him—but they were on such different paths now, weren't they?

If she didn't think she deserved Liam *then*, she certainly didn't deserve him *now*.

"I don't know how to fix us," she told the spirit. "To fix *me*."

The Ghost of Christmas Present turned to her. "If he's the one giving the love, and you're the recipient of it, isn't it up to *him* to decide if you're worthy of his affection?"

Carol looked at the ghost through blurred eyes. Her temple began to throb. This was suddenly too much—just *too* much. She couldn't solve the problems of the medical community, or mend all broken relationships. She was just one person.

Another painting of Liam's popped into her head. This one was a sphere of silver spinning on a lilac-colored lake beneath a teal sky. It was a painting he'd called *The Sphere of Influence*.

Everyone had their own sphere, Liam had explained to her—their own group of people, and their own environment, which they impacted both positively and negatively.

Whenever he got overwhelmed at all of the problems of the world, Liam had said he'd remind himself to scale his concerns down to his sphere of influence, who and what he could realistically improve without damaging or overwhelming his own psyche.

Maybe Carol could do that.

She couldn't change the dysfunctional, fractured medical system in this country, but she could change how she navigated through it.

The system might reward delayed, assembly-line care, but she didn't have to conform to that. Carol could add her own compassion at no cost to her. She could have a positive impact in her sphere of influence, even if nowhere else.

"I think I can do it. I think I know how to change."

The ghost gave Carol a beaming smile, and then he began to fade from the gallery.

"Then, you're already on your way to success," his voice lingered after him.

"Thank you for showing me the present."

The ghost dipped his head as he vanished.

· · ·

CAROL FOUND herself alone in the art gallery.

She stepped forward, wandering through the gallery until she vaguely noticed the scenery change around her. She blinked, shaking her head and looking around the new location.

She found herself in an apartment again, standing in a dark, unwelcoming living room.

In one corner, a towering figure, utterly unmoving and wearing a long, dark hood.

A chill ran down her spine and Carol shuddered at the sight of the Ghost of Christmas Future—Christmas Yet to Come.

He might as well be Death himself, or perhaps he was, because death was the inevitable outcome awaiting everyone.

Carol looked around the apartment again, fearing whose it might be—and what terrible future this ghost intended to show her.

Then, she saw them.

Johnny and his wife, crying together as they held a photograph of Corey in their hands.

Finally, Carol recognized the tiny apartment. It was theirs—but devoid of Christmas decorations, unlike the last time she'd seen it.

Carol's chest tightened. Surely, this hadn't happened— or didn't *have* to happen. This was a vision of the future, after all, and the future hadn't happened yet.

Corey just needed appropriate and timely treatment, that was all.

"No, no, no."

Carol spun away from the heart-breaking scene—only

to find herself back on the cold, dark streets of Chicago. This winter snow fell from a bleak sky, heavy with dark clouds.

She whirled around, back to face the Ghost of Christmas Yet to Come.

"Stop it! That won't happen. I won't *let* it happen."

The enormous cloaked figure said nothing. He only pointed a long, bony finger. Carol's gaze followed the direction he indicated.

She wiped tears out of her eyes and focused on a scraggly, weather-beaten man huddled in an oversized, stained coat. He was leaning against the wall of an abandoned storefront, with an unshaven beard and dirt-caked fingernails. His eyes looked distant and destitute.

Two women stopped to stare at him before continuing on their walk.

"I heard he was a famous painter, until he stopped painting one day." One of the women whispered to the other, her voice audible as the women passed where Carol was standing. "He traded his brushes for booze until he went broke…"

Carol shook her head, turning back to the homeless man. She recognized him through the dark beard; although not as the man she'd seen on Christmas Eve.

"No," Carol breathed. "Not Liam."

She turned back to the ghost, desperately grabbing hold of his abundant black robes. She looked up into the void of his faceless black hood.

"It doesn't have to be this way," Carol pleaded. "Let me fix it. I can save him—the way he saved me."

Carol turned toward the homeless man—her Liam.

She reached him, kneeling down to touch his bundled figure...

...and, instead, falling straight through the now-intangible sidewalk.

Carol screamed, plummeting into nothing. She fell through the darkness and landed roughly on her hands and knees, kneeling in soft dirt.

She struggled up to her feet, spinning around to face walls of dirt in every direction. Then, she looked up—at the rim of the six-foot deep hole she'd fallen into.

Looming down above her, she saw a tombstone.

DR. CAROL SULLIVAN

Above her on one side stood the large, hooded figure.

On the other stood Johnny, dressed in a black suit with Penny beside him.

High above, a gray sky hung heavy with clouds. Down in the pit—her own grave—Carol felt frigid with fear.

"Why did we come here?" Penny asked, looming over Carol's grave.

"Somebody had to," Johnny replied. "After all, she was my boss. She helped some people."

"As long as she was helping herself."

Johnny didn't refute that. Instead, he looked down into the grave and murmured: "Goodbye, Carol."

Then, the couple turned and walked away from her grave, leaving Carol alone in the darkness.

She wasn't alone for long. Someone else approached. Carol looked up and saw her sister standing at the edge of the grave.

She gulped.

Melanie didn't look much older than she was now, which meant...

Carol turned and looked up at the looming, black figure of Christmas Yet to Come. She longed to ask him: "When is this supposed to happen?"

But she knew he wouldn't answer her—and, in truth, she didn't need him to. She knew the answer.

Soon, apparently.

With tears in her eyes, Melanie dropped a single red rose into the grave. It fell, landing in the dirt at Carol's feet—the pedals scattering their crimson colors, in contrast to the black earth beneath them.

When Melanie left, someone began shoveling dirt into the grave.

Carol pressed herself against one wall of moist dirt as more cascaded down around her.

"Mel," she called up, out of the grave. "Mel, wait! Come back!"

Carol then turned toward the other side of the grave, where the Ghost of Christmas Yet to Come and his shabby black cloak towered over her. She tried to claw her way out of the deep, dark hole, but she couldn't find purchase in the moist dirt.

"Wait!" she cried. "I know what I have to do! I know how to change! Please!" She slipped and fell, landing on her back with a thud.

The dirt kept coming. Shovel-load after shovel-load, scooped up with the grating of metal against dirt.

"No!" Carol screamed.

Then, all fell silent.

CHAPTER 7

*C*arol opened her eyes.

She was lying on her back in her bed, tangled in her bedsheets and still wearing her jeans and sweater.

I'm alive.

She scrambled to the edge of the bed and snatched her phone off the charging station.

6 A.M. DECEMBER 25

Christmas day!

She stumbled out of bed and across the hallway into her home office. There, she logged onto her computer. In rapid succession, she sent several emails. Then, she ordered pre-cooked entrees and sides to be delivered in the afternoon. Next, she found the gallery website where Liam's work was showcased.

After making her purchases, Carol dashed to the bath-room, feeling like she was floating on a cloud of elation. She was alive—so full of life—and she knew what she needed to do.

After freshening up, she grabbed her purse and

hospital badge. Standing on the curb outside her brownstone, Carol inhaled crisp, chill air—the best kind, after a fresh snowfall. She caught a cab to the hospital.

En route, she called Jeff, one of the hospital financial officers.

"Carol, it's Christmas day." His voice crackled with irritation and exasperation. "Is there some financial crisis at the hospital?"

"Merry Christmas, Jeff."

"Uh, Merry Christmas," he replied uncertainly.

"I need a Christmas miracle," Carol said firmly. "Johnny has been my physician assistant for five years. He needs a Christmas bonus—a good one. That, and a raise—effective January 1st. He's underpaid, based on national averages, factoring in his experience and the cost of living for Chicago."

"You're telling me this now? Today?"

"A Christmas miracle, Jeff. I need you to make this happen."

"Carol…" he started to protest.

"Don't give me the company line about budget cuts and lean margins," Carol cut him off. "We've underpaid Johnny for far too long. Whenever he figures that out, he'll leave us for a job that pays him what he's worth. If I lose Johnny, my work productivity will fall by half until we hire and train a replacement. We both know that's a six to twelve-month endeavor, which is a much bigger loss than treating our employees as they ought to be treated."

"Okay, okay," Jeff sighed, "I can do the raise by January, but I can't release bonus funds on a holiday."

"I'll get him the bonus, and you can reimburse me," Carol replied. "I'm also doing one pro-bono case per month, starting in January."

"Carol…"

"Get behind it, Jeff. I'll get key administrators in a meeting after the holidays. They can spin it for marketing promotion if they want, but it's happening."

"What's gotten in to you, Carol? I thought you despised Christmas."

"I found the Christmas spirit I'd lost." She paused. "Oh, and I'm not working Christmas next year." Then, she hung up the phone, paid the cab fair, and bounded into the hospital.

Alive! Carol felt positively alive!

She passed nurses, aides, and other physicians—greeting them all with a "Merry Christmas!" Some stared in shock, while others smiled and returned the wish for a pleasant holiday.

Carol walked into Mr. Smith's room. He was sitting on the edge of his bed, eating breakfast in his faded blue hospital gown.

"Mr. Smith, you're looking well."

"Dr. Sullivan!" His unshaven face brightened. "Visiting on Christmas day?"

"I wanted to see how you're feeling. Your surgery went well, and I see your chest tube is out now. We should be able to get you home today."

"Today? That'd be a great Christmas present! The grandkids were hoping to visit this evening."

After a few minutes of socializing, Carol bid Mr. Smith a good day.

Next, she went to the ICU. When she reached Mr. Johnson's room, she found his family—wife and daughter —seated in his room. Carol pulled up a chair and sat in front of them.

"Dr. Sullivan?" the wife asked, startled.

Carol leaned forward looked deep into Mrs. Johnson's glistening eyes.

"I'm so sorry this happened to your husband."

"You told us pneumonia could happen."

"I know," Carol nodded, "but I wish this surgery would have worked for him."

"He hoped so, too, but he didn't want to live barely able to breathe. He'd rather die trying to get a better quality of life than live struggling the way he was."

Carol nodded. Mr. Johnson had told her the same thing before his operation, and she'd been honest about the risks of the surgery.

"I'm sorry it didn't work," Carol repeated. "I'm sorry he didn't recover—that he won't recover."

"He didn't want to linger on life support."

"I know. Whenever you're ready, we'll let him pass comfortably."

Mrs. Johnson gave a pained sigh. "He's ready. Let's let the grandchildren say goodbye tomorrow. After Christmas—tomorrow."

"Tomorrow," Carol echoed. "I'll be here, and we'll do it together."

AFTER CAROL LEFT THE HOSPITAL, she grabbed a cab and

stopped briefly at a department store on the way to Johnny's apartment.

With gift bag in hand, she slid out of the cab. "Keep the meter running," she called to the driver, before bounding up the stairs and knocking on Johnny's door.

Johnny answered the door in his pajamas, holding a cup of coffee. His eyes widened when he saw her. "Dr. Sullivan?"

"Merry Christmas, Johnny." She handed him the sparkling, silver bag.

"Johnny? Who's there?" Penny came to the door. At the sight of Carol, her expression darkened.

"Honey," Johnny said quickly, "Dr. Sullivan brought us a Christmas gift—isn't that *nice* of her?"

Penny's expression softened into confusion.

Carol extended a hand. "I'm Carol. We've never met, and that's inexcusable on my part."

Johnny pulled the card out of the bag and passed the bag to Penny.

"That's your bonus, Johnny," Carol explained, as he opened it. "That, and back payment on prior Christmas bonuses. There's also a letter in there, outlining your raise, effective January 1st."

Johnny stood there, eyes wide.

Carol turned to Penny.

"In the bag are a few Xbox games, and a gift card for more games for Corey. Penny, I bought you some scarves —because we don't know each other well enough for me to know what you like, but I hope to change that."

Johnny opened the envelope and gasped at the number on the check inside.

"Penny, look at this."

He showed it to her. Her mouth fell open.

Carol backed away toward the door.

"I have to go—more deliveries to make—but I hope you'll come this evening to my house for Christmas dinner. The invitation should be in your email."

Carol then turned and scurried down the stairs. She nearly tripped on the bottom one, catching herself and laughing at her own clumsiness.

Once back in the cab, she directed the driver to Melanie's apartment.

The cab pulled up, and Carol paid the driver. She grabbed her bag and strode into the apartment complex.

When Carol knocked on the door to her sister's apartment, Pike answered—with disheveled morning hair and stubble on his jaw.

He scratched his chin. "Carol? This is a pleasant surprise. Come on in."

Carol stepped inside, dropping the gift bag on the floor. She hugged her brother-in-law, and his posture stiffened in surprise.

"Thank you for being so good to Mel," Carol breathed, pressing her head against his broad chest.

"Carol?" Melanie walked into the room, eyes widening.

"Mel!" Carol's heart soared to see her sister. She rushed to hug her, and, just as quickly, she spun around and picked up the gift bag, thrusting it toward her sister.

"I bought baby stuff," Carol explained. "All gender neutral—but it's a start." Her eyes sparkled. "And I bought two of everything."

Melanie's eyes widened even further. "But how could you *possibly* know?"

Carol didn't answer. Instead, she continued: "And if you're not otherwise engaged, come to my Christmas dinner tonight." Then, Carol hugged Melanie again. "It's so good to see you."

With that, Carol abruptly turned and headed toward the door. She had one more stop to make before going back to her house to prepare for Christmas dinner.

"Wait!" Melanie ran after her, snatching a small box from under her tree. "Take your gift, but we *will* see you later, too."

Carol graciously accepted the box, which she recognized instantly.

She smiled but didn't open the gift.

"Thank you, Mel. It's one of my favorite photos. A perfect gift."

Leaving the couple pleasantly flabbergasted, Carol strode out of their apartment building and down the stairs to the street.

She pulled her coat tighter around her and breathed the air in deeply one more time. She'd go to The Stardust Gallery next, hoping to find Liam—*if* he checked his email and *if* he wanted to show up.

Ten minutes later, a cab dropped Carol outside the gallery. She walked up to the door, but could already see through the glass that the lights were off.

Well, it was mid-morning on Christmas, so perhaps

Liam hadn't checked his email after all. Alternatively—and sadly, more probable—he just didn't want to see her.

She couldn't blame him.

Carol tested the door. Locked. She peered inside and saw no movement within.

Turning, Carol walked back toward the street, one foot in front of the other. She was within walking distance of her brownstone now, but the need to see Liam overwhelmed her.

There was so much to make up for. She didn't know if he'd ever forgive her but she needed to try.

Cars zipped up and down the street. Carol neared the curb.

She swallowed and resolved not to give up on what she and Liam had. She'd check her email and see if he replied. Perhaps he had, and perhaps they could set up another rendezvous.

Still, as Carol pulled her phone from her pocket, she couldn't help but feel disappointment worm its way into her mind.

She reached the curb and extended her right leg to step down...

"Carol!" A cheerful male voice called to her.

Carol turned, paused mid-step. Then, she pulled her foot back and turned toward the sound of the voice—Liam.

As she pivoted toward him, a delivery truck barreled past her on the road—buffeting her and blasting cold air through her hair.

At the sight of Liam's smile, Carol barely even noticed the gush of wind from the truck hurtling past her. Instead, she walked toward him—barely resisting the urge to run into his arms.

Liam wore a cream-colored sweater and a fur-lined leather jacket. His dark hair was combed sleekly back, and his dark eyes twinkled with something like anticipation.

"Are you the 6 a.m. buyer, by any chance?"

"Yes," Carol grinned. "I *had* to have it."

In addition to sending several emails that morning, Carol had also finally purchased the horse painting—and a few others from the online store of The Stardust Gallery.

Liam smiled at her. "You lost sleep over it?"

She swallowed. "I lost sleep over you." A sense of vulnerability closed around her. The way she'd treated him, Liam had every right to lash out at her now.

"Over *me*?"

"Over *us*," she amended, her voice shaky. "I never should have let you go, Liam. Can you forgive me?"

His lips parted in a welcoming smile. "Carol, I forgave you the moment I saw you desperate to open the gallery doors on Christmas morning."

She leaned closer, arched up, and kissed him.

The kiss was as wonderful as she'd remembered—sweet and sensual, delicious and delightful, heavenly and homecoming. His kiss was Christmas—magical and miraculous.

When they broke away, she no longer felt cold and her loneliness melted away.

"What changed?" Liam asked, tucking her into his arms.

"Everything."

❄

TONY SAT on Carol's counter, unseen by all as he watched Christmas dinner unfold at her home. He'd only been granted that one moment to speak to her, when Carol had seen him on Christmas Eve. That would never happen again, according to the Christmas Spirits. Considering how badly he'd scared her, it was probably a good thing.

Tonight, he couldn't help but grin at the sight of so much holiday cheer. Carol's dining room was filled with green, red, and gold decorations—candles, miniature trees, and napkins. The table bowed beneath a Christmas turkey, green beans, mashed potatoes, buttered bread rolls, cranberry sauce, cornbread stuffing, and more. Tony wished he could smell all those delicious scents, mixed with the pumpkin pie baking in the oven.

Melanie, Pike, and Penny were busy bringing serving spoons to the table—while Johnny poured wine into waiting glasses. Corey snuck a bread roll while no one was looking.

In the kitchen, Liam and Carol couldn't keep their hands off each other. Carol couldn't stop smiling. Tony had never seen her so happy.

"Mission accomplished," Burke said, shimmering into manifestation beside Tony.

"Better than that," Tony grinned. "She's happy, changed, *and* still alive."

"The spirit of Christmas wins again, thanks to the Christmas Spirits."

"I got my Christmas miracle," Tony beamed.

"That you did."

Tony looked down at his arms and legs. "Whoa! What's happening?" He was growing even more translucent than he already was.

"You're moving on, Tony," Burke smiled. "Your spirit is at peace."

"Oh? Great! Wait." Tony's eyes widened. "What about you?"

"I've got my own unfinished business. Don't worry about me."

"See you in the next world, Burke?"

"See you, Tony."

ONE YEAR LATER

Carol fluffed the pillows and poured the wine, excited for Liam's arrival home. He was finishing up at the gallery charity auction and was due back at any moment.

His painting of the horses hung above the fireplace. To his delight, she'd redecorated her brownstone living room last January to match the colors and beauty of the painting.

Rediscovering their love had happened so seamlessly that they were already married come springtime. They'd honeymooned in Alaska. Carol had then cut back her work hours to a normal, full-time load—and she now spent most weeknights and weekends with her husband. They sailed Lake Michigan, walked through the parks together, and kissed at every opportunity, as if they were teenagers, instead of in their forties.

Melanie had given birth to two adorable twin girls— and soon after, Carol had begun making time to give the new mom a regular weekend break, babysitting for a few hours so Melanie could indulge in some much-needed self-care.

Meanwhile, Pike spoiled the twins with every female superhero outfit and action figure he could find, which was a lot of them.

Corey had finished cancer treatments, and his last bone marrow biopsy showed complete remission. Johnny and Penny had dinner with Carol and Liam once a month. Usually, the men cooked while Carol and Penny had long discussions over what wine paired best with the food.

When Carol heard the door unlocking, she walked over to greet Liam. He entered with a flourish, spinning her in a circle with one hand wrapped around her waist, and a hungry kiss pressed against her lips. He pulled her against him as he spun her around, still kissing her senseless.

"Liam," Carol said breathlessly, between kisses, "what's in your other hand?"

Reluctantly, he pulled away.

"Your Christmas gift," he pulled his arm behind his back, "but I know when I give it to you, you're going to neglect me, so I had to get my affections in first."

"What is it?" She laughed, trying to peek around to see what he had hidden behind his back.

Liam surrendered and thrust a squirming ball of fur at her.

"I'm not sure what he is—some type of mutt. He's a rescue, and the newest member of our family."

Carol sunk both hands into the puppy's soft, golden fur. He waggled an excited tail.

"He's adorable!" Carol inspected him as she petted the

squirming pup. "Definitely some Terrier. Maybe miniature Poodle and Schnauzer mix?"

Liam brought the puppy close to his face, and they nuzzled noses. "I think adorable covers it."

Carol took the puppy in her hands, and he licked them enthusiastically. "He's wonderful."

"What should we name him?"

"Something that's *us*," she pondered. "We met at Michigan Avenue—the Christmas tree."

"By Wrigley Square."

Carol smiled. "Wrigley!"

Liam grinned and leaned in for another kiss. "Wrigley? I like that."

"Come here, you." She tugged Liam closer—until there was no space between their bodies. "I'll never neglect you."

"Really? Let's have that glass of wine—and then you spend the night not neglecting me."

"I can do that."

Liam dipped his head for another kiss. "I love you."

"I love you, too."

STELLA'S STAR

Stella Maddox wakes in a remote cabin surrounded by strangers. And worse, she has no memory of who she is or how she arrived here—aside from following a mystery light in the shape of a star.

When Warner Orion takes his family on a winter getaway, he never imagined a woman would crash Christmas morning. But with the snowfall the day prior, the mystery woman isn't leaving anytime soon.

As they make the most of the Christmas holiday and work to recover Stella's memories, danger lurks on the mountain and the clock's ticking. Can Stella remember who she is in time to save the Orion family?

CHAPTER 1

The rapid wipers squeaked against the windshield as Stella struggled to see the road. Snow fell from the sky, giving the appearance she was encased inside a snow globe on a dark night.

She tensed, remaining ramrod straight and too focused to blink as she navigated the storm. With good weather, she was fifteen minutes from her parents' house, but in this mess, it might take her thirty.

The small puppy in the cushioned crate beside her whined softly.

"I know, Bandit. It's ugly out there."

One of the front wheels jolted, striking the edge of the road, or perhaps a pothole. The car started to slide on a slick patch of ice, but she kept the wheels straight without panicking, and the tires reconnected with the asphalt. She accelerated slowly, hoping to make it safely home.

Suddenly, a red pickup truck came toward her, driving down the middle of the highway. When she swerved to avoid a head-on collision, her car spun on an icy patch.

Life advanced in slow motion as her vehicle plummeted off the side of the road towards a tree. Every muscle in her body tensed.

She braced for impact and heard the crunch of metal as the airbag smacked her in the face.

Slightly dazed, she watched the headlights of her Subaru illuminate an enormous tree trunk. With a slightly tremulous grip on the wheel, she tried to restart the car. Nothing happened when she pushed the start button—not that she could drive her Impreza up the side of the hill through the snow drift anyway.

Beside Stella, Bandit whined.

"You need the bathroom, little guy? Okay, you pee, and I'll phone for help." She took him out of his car tote, thankful he'd been strapped in securely and was unharmed. Pulling on her hat and gloves, she braved the cold.

After he turned a patch of ice yellow, she picked him back up and tucked him into her coat for protection.

Grimacing, she inspected the caved-in front of her blue car. Yup, the only way it was moving now was with a tow truck. She pulled out her phone—no signal. She held it high as she walked in a circle around the car, a futile gesture, she knew. The storm must have been interfering with a tower or repeater.

"C'mon. Give me a signal," she willed, to no avail.

Frigid air blew around her as snow continued to pour from the sky. Taking in the surrounding darkness, she saw no lights in the distance. She knew cabins were sprinkled around the mountainside, but she could walk a mile and not find one if she went the wrong direction. She could stay in her car, but it wasn't likely to be spotted from the road. What she wouldn't do was panic. She'd been trained for harsh conditions and knew survival techniques.

She tapped her phone as she stared at the lack of service bars. She walked several steps in search of a mobile signal. This was certainly not how she'd intended to spend Christmas Eve. She'd hoped after last year's not-so-merry-and-bright holiday this one would be better. That didn't seem to be the case.

When her boot hit a slick stone jutting up from the snow, she pitched forward, and her phone flew from her hand. She curled her arms around Bandit, still under her coat, to protect him as she tumbled down the embankment.

TWELVE HOURS EARLIER

WARNER MOVED the mouse cursor along the computer screen as he tweaked his *Introduction to Solar Systems* PowerPoint-based lecture. Forty-two slides. At one minute per slide for the presentation, he would leave eighteen minutes of class time for questions. Except, students typically liked to end five minutes early, which meant he had left thirteen minutes for questions. However, if he added a few slides and shortened it to nine and a half minutes, he could point out how they had as many minutes for questions as Saturn was from the sun in astronomical units.

When he finished, he opened a browser window about local news. A front was moving in, bringing colder weather and snow. Perfect for playing outside on Christmas day. He skimmed through politics and celebrity news until an article caught his attention.

> JAIL BREAK. Six hours ago, Willie and Alvin Green broke out of the Virginian Corrections Department. Police have cast a wide net to search for the escaped convicts. The brothers were last seen in a red Chevy Colorado heading west.

A picture separating the text showed two large and unfriendly faces glaring at the camera. They wore orange jumpsuits and looked as different as two brothers could—one tall and thick, the other short and thin.

> The brothers were convicted of armed robbery and had served three of their eight-year sentence. Police cautioned that they are armed and dangerous.

> Can authorities catch the criminals, or will the Grinch Brothers ruin Christmas?

"Daddy, no working on Christmas Eve."

Warner shut the laptop before Lizzy could see the screen and scrubbed a hand along his face. "You're right, sweetie. I'm sorry."

What else could he say? He had work, and he had Lizzy. If she was busy with her dolls or sleeping in the early morning hours, all he knew to do was work.

"Come here, you." He helped her into his lap as he sat in a nook in the living room of the cabin he'd rented. Her golden curls tickled his nose as she leaned back.

He couldn't think of a more perfect moment—his six-year-old daughter curled against him as they looked at the winter wonderland outside the window with the sun rising over the horizon. In one of the bedrooms, his parents began stirring. Soon they'd be up and making breakfast for the family.

He basked in the serene moment with Lizzy. He could get used to enjoying a view like this as he worked, though he might catch himself daydreaming more.

After the expected snow tonight, their location and the weather would make the perfect holiday; tomorrow, they could spend Christmas morning playing in the soft white powder right outside their front door. He needed to enjoy the vacation and maximize their quality time together.

Lizzy turned and looked up at him. "Do you want to have a tea party for breakfast?"

He chuckled. She wasn't capable of sitting still for more than a minute and enjoying a beautiful moment, but that was okay; he would relish whatever little tender morsels he could.

"I'd love a tea party!" He tickled her as they stood.

❄

STELLA HELD her plank pose as she gazed out the window at the snow-covered ground—a picturesque scene on Christmas Eve with more snow to come later tonight. Out here in the hills of remote Virginia, everything was quiet and tranquil. This was exactly what she'd needed to soothe her soul.

When the oven buzzed, indicating it had reached her desired temperature, she counted out her last five push-ups and stood, adjusting her long sweater over her yoga pants.

A ball of fur tumbled across her bare feet.

"Hello, Bandit." She scooped up the puppy and nuzzled her nose in the soft fur of her newest best friend.

The mixed breed husky and Australian Shepherd squirmed playfully.

"You need to go outside, don't you?"

She slipped the sheet of a dozen cookies into the oven before tugging on her winter coat and wool-lined boots to brave the cold. The fresh mountain air was crisp and raised her holiday spirit.

The slick walkway presented a hazard as she carried Bandit, but she gingerly made her way to a small clearing of wilted grass she'd shoveled clear earlier. She set down the puppy who took care of business.

Back inside, she took off her boots and coat and washed her hands. Bandit chewed a rope, and warmth flooded her at the smell of baking cookies. A low-key Christmas with just her and man's best friend would be sheer bliss.

When her mobile phone cut through the silence, she put the call on speakerphone. "Hi, Mom. Your house is fine—still in one piece."

"I was calling to check on *you*."

"I'm great. I always love this place in the winter. It's the perfect Christmas location, and I can't believe you aren't staying here over the holidays to enjoy it." Stella also couldn't believe her parents hadn't even put up a Christmas tree this year.

When she'd arrived three days ago to take on the role of house-sitting, she'd commented on the lack of decorations. Her mother had explained that since they were traveling to the Caribbean, putting up a tree only to take it back down when they came home seemed like a waste of time.

"Sweetheart, we're in a tropical paradise with eighty-degree weather. Next year we'll have a nice get together at the house. Is that mutt of yours behaving himself?"

"I promise I'm keeping a close eye on him. When you get back, you won't find a single carpet stain or chewed shoe."

Little Bandit had an array of toys to cut his teeth on, and Stella had been letting him out regularly to house train him.

"Oh, I wish you had found a man instead of a dog." Her mother gave a wistful sigh.

"Yeah, well, dogs don't cheat and lie."

"There are a lot of good men out there."

"And I'm convinced they're all taken. But that's okay. I'm going to have a beautiful white Christmas in the company of my new best friend."

Stella had convinced herself that she cheerfully anticipated Christmas alone. Isolation would be cleansing after the heart-wrenching events of last Christmas. She could have a drama-free holiday and think of all the ways the new year would be a new beginning. She hadn't bothered to date over the last year due to a combination of her past experience shattering her trust in men and lack of opportunity as a result of her job travel schedule.

"Okay. Well, don't forget to scrape the driveway. There's another snowstorm coming, and it gets absolutely unmanageable if it's not cleaned daily."

"I've got your entire to do list here. And don't worry about calling and checking on me. I'm going to have a pleasant Christmas. You enjoy yours." Stella had plans to do some endurance training while in the mountains, and she'd brought her rifle for target practice. "Call me when your plane lands at Richmond to let me know you made it back safe."

"Merry Christmas, Stella."

"Merry Christmas, Mom."

Stella set down her phone and walked through her parents' house to the utility drawer in the kitchen. She thought putting up a few Christmas decorations would solidify her holiday spirit but couldn't remember where her mom kept the attic key and had forgotten to ask before they'd hung up.

She rummaged through the kitchen drawer with scissors, pens, paper clips, screwdrivers, a stapler, rubber bands, and other odds and ends. She didn't find a key.

She then walked to her parents' bedroom and opened the door. Perhaps there was a place in here where the key was stored. Her gaze fell on her mother's jewelry box on the dresser. She'd always adored the polished mahogany wood with intricate carvings.

Fun memories of trying on her mother's jewelry as a child danced in her mind. She would wear one of her mom's silk shirts as a dress, slip on a pair of high heels much too big for her, and then don necklaces and rings. Her mom would laugh and photograph her all decked out. As an adult, though, Stella didn't have a lifestyle with any need for nice clothing and expensive jewelry.

She ran her hand over the smooth surface of the jewelry box and lifted it open, admiring the sparkling silver and gold. The contents of the box were like Christmas themselves. Then, she saw her mom's engagement ring, and the large and opulent piece of jewelry winked at her. Stella knew her mom had left it at home so as not to risk losing it on her Caribbean dream vacation.

Stella's own engagement ring had been simpler, though all the details were difficult to recall since she'd worn the cursed thing less than twenty-four hours before throwing it back in Chuck's face.

She picked up her mother's ring and slipped it on. The fit was a little snug. It would certainly look odd wearing a diamond on her left hand while holding an M18 Sig in her right. She turned her wrist left and right, admiring the way the sun through the bedroom window made the diamond dazzle.

But love wasn't an expensive ring—the fickle emotion contained nothing so solid and pure. Maybe that's why diamonds were a girl's best friend—jewelry couldn't betray you.

She would have taken true love over a diamond ring any day. Foolish dreams. She tugged at her mother's ring to remove it, intending to put it back, but it didn't budge.

Uh, oh.

Nothing a little soap wouldn't fix.

Her phone alarm went off, signaling the cookies were finished baking.

When she returned to the kitchen, the aroma of cinnamon filled the air as Stella pulled the snickerdoodle cookies out of the oven. They were a perfect golden brown. *Oh, but the ensemble is only perfect when coupled with eggnog.* She checked the refrigerator.

Shoot. No nog.

Out the window, a clear sky spread above the trees. More snow was expected later today, but she should be able to travel to the store and back before the precipitation started. It was now or never, since none of the local stores would be open on Christmas day.

She turned off the oven, bundled up, and stepped outside with Bandit. As she set to work shoveling the short driveway, the puppy played in the snow—jumping, spinning, and snapping at the cold, white piles.

Manual labor. This was excellent. And it did wonders to distract her from dwelling on last year's debacle.

A cracking and snapping of plastic brought her attention back to the present. The snow shovel had fractured at the handle, rendering it useless.

"Add snow shovel to the list." She set it aside. "Apparently, I don't know my own strength."

Fortunately, she had cleared most of the drive—

enough to make it to the road. Next, she layered down the salt in case the snow fell before she returned.

Quick trip. Eggnog, shovel, and... now, rock salt.

To be thorough, she went back through the fridge and pantry and made a list. Next, she secured Bandit in the passenger seat beside her in a cushioned crate lashed to the seat by the seatbelt. His tongue lolled out, happy as a lark to be in the car.

Maybe she should get dog biscuits, too.

In the car, her phone rang, and she put the call on speaker.

"Stellaaaa!" her brother bellowed.

She rolled her eyes even as she smiled to herself. "Yeah, because that never gets old. Hello, Mark." She doubted he'd even seen *A Streetcar Named Desire*. She pulled out of the drive and onto the road, intending to go to the hardware store first.

"How are you?" he asked.

Apparently, her entire family was checking up on her before Christmas. Probably because they'd had to deal with her morose mood for the first six months of the year following last Christmas's sorrow. But a few hours every day at the gun range and judo sparring had mostly cleared her mind of the devastation.

"All tucked in at mom's place," she said. "I'll have a cozy Christmas with my new dog and snickerdoodle cookies."

"And eggnog?"

"You know it."

"I wished you'd have come to our family Christmas," Mark said.

"I'm ready for some *me* time."

She also didn't want the inevitable looks of sympathy from extended family that she was still single after a break up a year ago or—heaven forbid—the dreaded, *'he wasn't good enough for you, anyway.'* While the statement was true, the words offered no real consolation when she considered how long they'd been together, only to have the sudden realization that the relationship had all been a terrible waste of time and emotion.

"Uh-huh. You sure you're not up to some secret spy mission?"

"I'd tell you, but then I'd have to… you know."

Mark laughed. "Yeah, yeah. Okay, enjoy your *supposed* Christmas alone. You know, with all your connections, you could have made Chuck's life miserable. Made him suffer."

"He doesn't get to have me. That's his punishment."

"Then he's definitely missing out."

Stella chuckled.

"Merry Christmas," her brother said.

"Backatcha."

He disconnected the call, and she knew the next time they'd talk would be to exchange Happy New Year greetings.

Mark always excelled at lifting her spirits. And somehow, he saw through her false bravado, knew when she was hurting, and knew just what to say without making her admit weakness.

In truth, she blamed herself for what happened as much as Chuck. They'd been dating for five years when she had finally stopped dropping hints and told him she wanted a commitment. A month later, he'd tossed a box to her from across the room with a hearty, "Your wish has been granted." The cavalier proposal was hardly the delivery she'd expected. It was devoid of magic, but she'd told herself she'd asked for the commitment, not the romance. If she'd wanted romance, perhaps she should have specified that as well.

The next day, on a surprise visit to his apartment, she'd found him in bed with a scantily clad Miss Claus asking him how naughty he planned to be. Stella considered her character one of cool under pressure; all the same, it was probably best she hadn't been wearing her sidearm at the time.

She blamed herself for ignoring warning signs and nudging Chuck in a direction he wasn't ready to go. Yet, she'd invested five years in their relationship. Five long years. At least she'd learned the truth before she wore more than an engagement ring.

The hardware store visit was uneventful—in and out with a shiny new shovel and a five-pound bag of driveway salt. And she even found a sprig of real mistletoe for sale. She bought it—not because she nurtured any delusions she would put it to good use—but because her parents would enjoy the sight of it when they arrived home from vacation. She even knew where she'd put it—under the little decorative arch in the foyer.

The first grocery store she reached had an empty parking lot. The sign on the door read CLOSED for inclement weather.

She looked up at the darkening sky. Only one more store. If it was closed, she would tuck her tail and go home without eggnog.

A few miles down the road, the first white flakes began their descent. But that wasn't a problem—temperatures weren't freezing yet. Maybe the precipitation would hit the road and melt. Melt and then freeze into ice on the surface by sunset?

No worries. She would be home before that happened.

CHAPTER 2

"What if Santa doesn't find us because we're not at home?"

"Oh, don't worry about that. He'll find us." Warner stroked a hand through his daughter's soft curls as he tucked her in for the night. They'd had a fun day of tea parties, snuggling with stuffed animals, and reading books. "You remember the story of the Christmas Star I told you?"

"The three wise men couldn't have followed a normal star to baby Jesus because no star matches the time and place of his birth."

He nodded. "That's right. It can't be explained by science—and yet, a guiding light took them where they needed to go. So, you see, Christmas is a time for miracles, and Santa will find us."

He knew that scientists speculated the star phenomenon had been three planets perfectly aligned, or perhaps a comet, but the theories hadn't been proven to the satisfaction of scholars, and so added to the magic of the story.

"Then why can't I have the present I want?" Lizzy asked, her tone infused with a longing whine.

Warner sighed, his heart breaking a little. "Because Santa doesn't deliver people for Christmas, only objects."

"Not even new moms?"

He pulled the covers tighter around her. They had already had this discussion two weeks ago when he'd read over her letter to Santa and had been flabbergasted to read her first request—a new mother. The second thing she wanted was a puppy.

Three years had passed since Lizzy's mother had died, and Warner hadn't started dating regularly yet. Work and being a single parent kept him plenty occupied. Dating would devour evening time he valued with Lizzy.

In addition, the idea of slugging through dozens of dates to find someone to forge the foundation of a relationship sounded daunting. And how many failed relationships would he have to endure to find the right woman who would love both of them?

"Not even new moms," he said definitively.

"The puppy then?"

"Puppies only go to homes with people who have time to care for them, sweetie." He had certainly not bought her a puppy for Christmas. A pet would have been another undertaking which would require entirely too much time and patience for a full-time working man and single father.

A knock came at the door.

"Gran!" Lizzy smiled.

"I'm just coming to say goodnight, dear. Tomorrow's the big day." Warner's mother entered and gave Lizzy a kiss on the forehead.

Warner watched the tender moment, happy his parents were able to join them on this holiday vacation. Sharing Christmas morning with them would make it all the more magical.

When his mother left, Lizzy asked, "Will you sing *We Three Kings?*"

"Of course." He relaxed against the headboard as Lizzy cuddled into her blankets, then, taking a breath, he softly began singing John Henry Hopkins's 1857 Christmas carol.

> *We Three Kings of Orient are,*
> *Bearing gifts we traverse afar,*
> *Field and fountain,*
> *Moor and mountain,*
> *Following yonder Star.*
>
> *O Star of Wonder, Star of Night,*
> *Star with Royal Beauty bright,*
> *Westward leading,*
> *Still proceeding,*
> *Guide us to Thy perfect Light.*

When he finished the song, he kissed her forehead softly and bid her goodnight. He would probably wait until around ten o'clock to set out the array of wrapped presents from Santa. Maybe some of them would be good enough to make his daughter forget her fanciful notion of having Santa bring her a mother.

SHE WOKE TO A THROBBING HEADACHE. Shivering violently, she struggled to focus on her surroundings. Bare trees towered over her, stretching up from a blanket of snow. All was shrouded in darkness with a sliver of moon intermittently visible behind briskly moving, heavy clouds.

When she sat up, her jacket moved, and a small head protruded.

"Well, hey there, cutie," she began, but she couldn't recall the puppy's name or if it even belonged to her.

Keeping the animal snuggled securely in her jacket, she pushed to her feet. She needed to get moving to avoid freezing to death.

But where was she?

Even more alarming—*who* was she?

Survival meant she couldn't dwell on what she didn't know or the throbbing pain at the back of her head. She needed shelter, and everything else was secondary to that.

She patted her pockets. No phone. No flashlight.

She pushed aside a feeling of despair and forced her legs forward through the snow.

Stay warm. Move.

She wouldn't give up and die in the wilderness. And if anything happened to her, this small animal—clearly under her care—wouldn't last long.

A twinkle in the distant sky caught her attention. Was it a star? It looked too low in the sky to be a star, but it wasn't moving like a plane. In fact, it was in front of the clouds, not behind them. Inexplicably, she felt drawn to the light and walked toward it.

The longer she stared, the more she realized the star blinked rather than twinkled. The series of blinks were specific and repeated over and over.

The light was communicating.

WARNER STOOD near the living room sofa, coffee cup in hand, and stared down at the woman sleeping on the couch. He couldn't fathom how she'd entered the cabin.

Christmas morning sunlight streamed through one window, casting a glow on the woman's peaceful, slumbering face. She was bundled in a winter coat with her hands tucked in her pockets.

He'd first noticed her when he'd passed through the living room on the way to the kitchen to make coffee. Since she'd been sleeping and didn't look particularly dangerous with her pink cap and puffy coat, he had proceeded to brew a pot and then check all the windows and doors.

Nothing appeared unlocked or displaced.

The main door of the rental property was keycode access only, so he wondered if there had been some mix-up with the rental office and this woman had thought she'd also rented the cabin. That logic was hard to justify since dual renter-ship didn't explain why she'd shown up in the middle of the night with no luggage and no visible vehicle outside.

Warner's mother and father filled their cups of coffee and joined him as all three of them stared at the sleeping beauty.

"Darnedest thing," his father, Ralph, said.

"If she was walking in that storm last night, it's a wonder she didn't freeze to death," said Louise, his mother.

Warner sipped his coffee. "I'm sure she'll have a logical explanation when she decides to wake up and enlighten us."

"You don't suppose she's in some type of unconscious state, more than just sleeping?" Ralph asked.

The intruder's coloring looked healthy, and her chest rose and fell with normal breathing. The mountain roads were impassible to vehicles after the storm. If she was injured, no aid could travel to or from the cabin until the snow cleared, so medical evaluation and care would have to wait. Before Warner could answer his father, Lizzy came bounding down the stairs.

She gasped when she saw the woman on the sofa. "Santa delivered a new mom!"

Warner blanched as his parents turned to gape at him. He cleared his throat. "No, honey," he began addressing Lizzy.

But the woman stirred, and all eyes turned toward her. She started to sit up but froze when she noticed the room full of people.

"Where am I?" she asked, wide-eyed.

"Don't look so frightened," Louise said. Her head full of gray curls probably looked the least threatening next to Warner's flannel pajamas and the stuffed unicorn in

Lizzy's grasp. "You maybe entered the wrong rental cabin. I'm sure it happens. I'm Louise, and this is my husband Ralph and our son Warner. That's our granddaughter Lizzy."

A yipping sound emitted from the woman as her coat moved. She startled before unzipping her coat to reveal a small, fluffy puppy.

"And Santa brought a puppy!" Lizzy declared.

Warner stared at the pair of them, speechless. The woman sat up, holding the puppy in her hands. He appeared to be part Husky.

"Oh, would you look at him? He must be starving." His mother lifted the puppy from the woman's hands and inspected him. "Who are you, Mr. Adorable?" She read his collar. "Bandit. Oh, my. That's rather ferocious, isn't it? Hardly befitting such a cute thing as yourself."

The dog licked her fingers enthusiastically as she petted him.

Ralph adjusted the coffee cup in his hand. "Why don't you tell us who you are, young lady? How can we get you where you belong? It's Christmas morning—someone must be very worried about you."

"Christmas!" The woman gasped as she reached around and gently touched the back of her head. "I don't know who I am. I don't know how I got here." She tugged off her cap, revealing a head of dark, glossy hair.

"Perhaps you have some identification," Warner said. He hated so see her so distraught.

When she looked up at Warner through dark lashes, his heart fluttered a few beats. He noticed an engagement ring on her finger as she fidgeted with her coat. Of course, she was married. She was youthful and pretty, probably late-twenties if he had to guess.

She stood up slowly, a little unbalanced, and unzipped her winter coat. She rummaged through multiple pockets in her coat and blue jeans but produced only a tube of Chapstick and a matchbook. "I'm sorry. I'm at a complete loss here. And I seem to have crashed your Christmas morning."

"Don't be sad," Lizzy stepped up and took her hand, staring up at her with big eyes. "Santa brought you. Maybe you're too new from the factory to have a memory."

The woman smiled warmly at Lizzy. "That's very sweet of you."

Warner set down his coffee cup and scooped Lizzy into his arms. "I'm sure Jane Doe didn't drop down the chimney, honey. But we'll sort it out."

Finding a beautiful woman in his living room on Christmas morning might have felt like a Christmas present if she hadn't also been sporting a two-carat diamond ring. Whomever she was attached to was probably losing his mind right about now.

"Jane?" Lizzy wrinkled her nose. "I don't think she looks like a Jane. We should give her a better name. Daddy, what's the name of your favorite galaxy?"

"Andromeda."

"Yes, let's call her that!"

The woman had beautiful eyes that he could just as easily star gaze into. All the more reason to *not* name her anything related to objects of his affection. He didn't know this woman and needed to keep his distance.

"Honey, when people don't remember their name, we call them Jane or John. It's very standard."

"You keep rubbing your head. Are you okay?" Ralph asked the woman.

"What about Star?" Lizzy suggested. "She's like our Christmas Star!"

"I've got a tender lump back there. I'm guessing I hit something, and that's why I can't remember who I am."

"If it's okay with her." Warner acquiesced to his daughter.

"Can we call you Star?" Lizzy asked her.

"Um. Okay. That's a very nice name."

"Don't fret about the memories, honey," Louise said as she ushered the woman into the kitchen. "You'll feel better with a strong cup of coffee and some food. While we're at it, we'll feed this little guy."

"I can help feed him!" Lizzy squirmed out of Warner's grasp and darted into her grandmother. "Star, can I feed your dog?"

"Yes. Thank you."

While the pair of them took care of the dog, Ralph worked at pulling eggs and bacon out of the refrigerator, and Warner walked over to the coffee machine.

Star. He liked the name a little too much, and it only added to the mysteriousness of her arrival.

Perhaps with some caffeine and nutrition, her memory would return to her, and she would be able to go back to where she belonged.

CHAPTER 3

S tar inhaled the scent of coffee.

Star.

The name didn't sound quite correct, but Star seemed better than no name at all.

"How do you like your coffee?"

She stared at Warner with his disheveled, dirty blond hair, bit of stubble, and incredibly warm eyes. Whenever she felt a rising panic at the thought of her amnesia, one look into those eyes grounded her.

How do you like your coffee? It seemed such an innocuous question—something you were asked at a restaurant by a complete stranger. But standing beside a man wearing pajamas in his kitchen, the offer felt personal and intimate. The room grew warm; she needed to take her jacket off—except she realized she already had.

"Star?"

"Black." Maybe he would think her delayed response was amnesia-related and not because she was thinking about what lay beneath the red and green flannel he wore.

He poured the beverage and offered it to her. She accepted with both hands, grazing his hand with hers.

A zing spread through her. When she looked up, Warner was close and looking down at her. His gaze skimmed from her eyes to her lips and down to the mug she held. They settled on her left hand a beat before he blinked and took a step back.

She looked at the hand. Right. Engagement ring. She was engaged.

She tried to grasp this bit of information to see if it would trigger other memories, but the only sensation rising to the surface was a sour, unsettled feeling, as if she teetered on the edge of darkness staring into an abyss.

The ring was too ostentatious; she was certain it wasn't suited to her taste. And it felt too snug. Had it not been sized correctly? Then again, something so expensive ought to be tight so it wouldn't risk being lost—especially if she was going to do more wandering around in the woods at night.

And if she was engaged, why did she wake in a cabin with no memory? Where was Mr. Right in all of this?

"Since the snow's abated," Warner told her, "I can walk around the cabin, maybe down to the road to see if I spot your car or mobile phone. If nothing turns up, we can call the police and see if anyone has filed a missing person's report."

"Thank you. I don't know if I'll ever be able to repay your generosity."

Warner smiled, a reassuring expression that sent yet another wave of warmth through her. Smiling revealed faint crow's feet around his brown eyes. She suspected he was late thirties in age.

How old was she? The answer didn't materialize.

"No, seriously," she said. "I don't even know if I have money, so I quite literally might not be able to pay you back."

He chuckled. "Let's focus on finding out who you are first. I saw you staring at the ring. Is it triggering anything?"

Something vile. It triggered anger and resentment and the urge to yank it off.

"No names." She looked away and drank more of her coffee.

"I guess we'll stick with Star for now."

"'What's in a name?'" she quipped. Though, truthfully, her whole identity might be out there, riding the wind on a name she needed only to remember.

Before she could swirl down a blackhole of anxious worry, Warner smiled again. She decidedly needed a colder beverage if she was going to have to endure his smile much longer.

"Can I have a look at your head?" he asked. "I saw you rubbing it a few minutes ago. With the weather, we can't get you any sort of timely medical care."

"Uh, sure." She turned around and put a finger to the lump on her scalp where the injury was.

He set down his coffee cup. With her back to him, she felt his fingers move her hair aside and gently palpate the skin. The tender contact sent gooseflesh rising along her arms.

"Does it hurt?"

She swallowed and shook her head. On the contrary, she could stand there for hours and let his hands roam her scalp.

"The wound isn't open. You might want some anti-inflammatories for the swelling."

She turned back around as Warner withdrew his hands.

"Thanks." She hoped he didn't notice the huskiness in her voice.

"I'm going to go..." His voice trailed as he blinked at her.

She'd been staring at him and probably made him uncomfortable. Their bodies were so close, she could see the gold flecks in his brown eyes. Had she forgotten her manners along with her identity?

He cleared his throat. "I'll go see if there are any trails indicating where you came from."

"I'll go with you." Wanting to get out of the house and into the cold in search of answers, Star placed her coffee cup on the table and prepared followed him.

She nearly ran into him when he abruptly turned back to look at her.

"That won't be necessary. You should take your clothes off." His eyes widened, and his lips formed a surprised 'O' at his own words. "I mean, they're filthy. It looks like you took a tumble in the dirt. You should stay here, warm up with coffee and a hot shower, and we'll find you some clean clothes while we wash these."

He stepped back from her as a flush spread into his cheeks. Looking away, he walked to the front door and slipped on his coat and goulashes before disappearing into a sea of white snow. Bandit followed him out the door.

When Star turned around, all eyes were focused on her. Warner's parents stood shoulder to shoulder, his father with a spatula in one hand and his mother with a stick of butter. As they stared at her with amused half-smiles, the hopeful twinkle in their eyes made Star uncomfortable.

She needed to get her memories back. "Can I help with anything?"

"No, I've got breakfast under control," Ralph said. "You just take it easy after that bump on the head. Ibuprofen is in that cabinet." He gestured.

"Lizzy dear, when your father gets back, we can open your presents," Louise said.

Star frowned, reminded that she was intruding on this family's picturesque Christmas morning. She needed her identity and a way to leave. She fetched the ibuprofen and took two with her coffee.

Lizzy sat down at the kitchen table. "I have more presents than just Star and a new puppy?" She turned to Star. "Did you come down the fireplace? Is that why you're dirty?"

Star smiled. "I wish I remembered." But she had dirt, not soot, on her pants and coat. And she did recall hiking through snow and frigid air on her way to this cabin.

Louise placed a gentle hand on her shoulder. "It'll come back, dear."

Ralph stirred scrambled eggs on the stovetop. "I read somewhere that trauma combined with stress can cause amnesia. Maybe the Christmas Spirit thought you needed a little stress relief. Something to temporarily forget your troubles."

"Like crashing someone else's Christmas?" Star chuckled. "I like Lizzy's idea. I'm actually a Santa factory robot, and I have no memories because I haven't made them yet." She started moving stiffly as if she was the tin man himself.

"Par-don me," Star said in her most robotic voice. "Would you like me to but-ter your toast for you?" She picked up a butter knife and then let her arm dangle at the elbow as if on a hinge.

Everyone laughed, and Star filled with instant satisfaction at her humor. Lizzy's giggle was especially heartwarming.

Yes, humor was Star's friend. That much she was sure. It was an excellent defense mechanism against the harshness of reality. Humor could bring people together and bridge common ground. Maybe she was a comedian. But that didn't feel right. Humor was a coping mechanism for her, not a career.

WARNER ENTERED the cabin and stared at his family's enjoyment of Star's humor as he held the puppy. He set Bandit on the carpet and closed the door behind him before shucking off his coat and boots.

Everyone turned to look at him expectantly.

"Nothing," he said. "Snow covered all tracks. There are no vehicles at the end of the drive near the road."

He had assumed she'd come by car, but a car accident

didn't explain the bump on the *back* of her head. Had something more dangerous happened to her last night?

"You should look on the roof," Lizzy said, "for sleigh tracks."

When he caught sight of Star's bright smile, he gave a lopsided grin.

"Breakfast is ready," Ralph announced.

"I'm still in my pajamas," Warner said.

"I still look like I rolled in mud," Star added.

Warner winced. He wished he hadn't fumbled his words like that earlier.

"Oh, none of us mind. You've been through an ordeal." Louise waved a hand.

After taking turns washing hands, the five of them sat around the table. Warner found himself sitting beside Star.

"This smells wonderful," she said. "I don't know when I ate last, but my stomach seems to think it's been at least a day." But she didn't move to take any food.

Not wanting her to remain hungry out of politeness, Warner filled each person's plate with eggs, bacon, and toast, including hers. "Let's hope we don't discover any food allergies you've forgotten about."

"Yes. That would be a bummer. I'm hungry enough to risk it. Any doctors or nurses in the vicinity?"

"Daddy's a teacher of astronomy!"

"*O star of wonder / star of light.*" Star looked around the table. "I don't know where that came from. I guess it's appropriate for the season."

"John Henry Hopkins. My favorite Christmas song, since it's about stars."

"Where do you teach?"

"University of Virginia. We're just renting this cabin for the holidays."

"Warner, Lizzy, Ralph, and Louise." Star pointed around the table to indicate each of them. "Seems my short-term memory is functional."

"We're the Orions," Ralph said.

"So, it's Professor Orion?" Star asked Warner.

"Warner is fine."

"We live in Charlottesville," Louise added.

"Except for my mom," Lizzy interjected. "She lives in heaven."

"Oh."

"Daddy says she went to be with the constellations three years ago. I don't remember her."

Warner patted Lizzy's shoulder.

Star swallowed a bite of bacon. "I remember seeing a beautiful star last night when I was wandering around in the cold. It shone particularly bright right over this cabin."

Warner ignored the inquiring glances his parents cast his direction. "Planets can seem like stars. This time of year, Saturn, Jupiter, and Mars can look bright in the night sky."

Lizzy nodded and swallowed a bite of eggs. "The first night we stayed at the cabin, Daddy and me looked at constellations—Perseus and Aries."

To avoid his family exploring the "star" their guest claimed to see, Warner seized the opportunity to launch into a dissertation about which constellations were best seen this time of year from the northern hemisphere.

*

AFTER BREAKFAST, Lizzy busied herself playing with Bandit, and Warner tried not to think about the tears that would flow when both Star and the puppy had to reunite with the rest of their family. Since his daughter was preoccupied with the ball of fur, he decided he would clean himself up before opening presents and give Star the same opportunity. His mother led her off into the unused room with a bathroom.

Warner dressed in blue jeans and a sweater before taming his bed head. After that, he called the local police station to ask if anyone had reported a missing woman. No one had. He left his number and Star's description so they could contact him when her fiancé started looking for her.

Warner instantly didn't like this man. Why hadn't he called the police yet? Was he waiting for the fabled twenty-four-hour missing person's rule invented by movie directors? If Warner had someone like Star in his life, he would have called the police after an hour of her unexplained absence, especially in a snowstorm and with escaped convicts on the loose. He thought about the bump on her head and wondered what—or who—had been responsible.

He scowled at the phone after he hung up. Authorities had been a dead end. And although Star seemed to be in good condition, she had a point about the availability of medical care. Since she'd hit her head hard enough to induce amnesia, she probably needed to be evaluated by a doctor.

But the roads might take a day or two to be cleared by the department of transportation. He should start shoveling the long driveway now, so he would be done by the time service vehicles finished the roads. It wouldn't do much good to have a drivable road with no driveway to get there.

An hour later, everyone convened in the living room where Lizzy tore at wrapping paper. Bandit seem to understand the object of the game was to shred paper, and so he dutifully did his part with small, sharp teeth. Star sat on the couch beside Louise, looking extremely entertained by his daughter and the puppy.

She wore clean clothes he suspected were his mother's —baggy jeans and a long sleeve T-shirt.

The woman's dark mahogany hair and bright blue eyes were a stunning contrast to each other. He'd stood a little too close to those eyes earlier. They were the sky on a cloudless day super imposed over space itself with sparkling stars and nebula in the background.

Andromeda eyes.

When his father nudged him, Warner realized he'd been staring at Star. He immediately turned his attention back to his daughter and her toys. If he wasn't careful, he'd end up becoming as attached to Star as Lizzy was, even though he'd only just met her, and his attraction defied logic.

CHAPTER 4

*A*fter present opening, Warner bundled up Lizzy and took her outside to play in the snow.

Star joined them, wearing his mom's coat while her clothes were in the washing machine. Bandit dutifully followed at her heel.

"I'm going to walk around and see if I can jostle any memories." She tugged her pink hat down over her head.

Warner suspected she wanted to look around for her phone and car for herself, which was a good idea since it might trigger some recollection.

He knelt down and helped Lizzy pile snow to build a snowman. Playing together reinforced how renting the cabin had been a great idea. He needed more time like this devoted to the two of them.

When Star returned from her unfruitful expedition, Lizzy invited her to join them for snowman building.

"Sure!" Star adjusted her gloves. "Maybe it will churn some memories to the surface. Perhaps I'm a talented sculptor, and when I create art, my amnesia will dissolve." She winked at Lizzy.

"Let's get to work, *Michelangelo*." Warner chuckled.

Together, the three of them rolled and packed snow in three large balls.

"I'm amazed how you're taking all of this in stride," Warner said.

"What do you mean?" Star asked.

"If I had knocked my head hard enough to wake somewhere with no memories, I'd probably be more distraught. Grown men have cried over less."

Star laughed as she packed in more snow to one of the balls. "That hardly seems productive. Anyway, these things take time, right? Besides, I crashed your Christmas. I would only make it worse if I moped and complained. And I could've frozen out there in the winter night, so I guess I'm feeling fortunate to be alive rather than unfortunate to not remember who I am. Some might even call my present state a miracle."

"A Christmas miracle? You're a cup half-full kind of woman." Warner picked up the middle of the snowman and placed it on top of the larger sphere on the ground.

"I think I'm more of an add-more-to the-cup-if-you're-not-happy-with-the-fluid-level kind of woman."

"I like that." Warner enjoyed Star's easy presence. Her smile and warm voice lightened any mood.

He recalled himself having a better sense of humor once upon a time. When Lizzy was a baby, he'd excelled at making her smile and giggle. He'd been the playful dad whose wife had demanded he parent more and play less. After she'd passed, he'd become more like the father she'd asked of him. But Lizzy needed moments like today in her life, and he needed to do better enriching their quality time with joy. Building a snowman was a start.

Star lifted the head of the snowman and placed it securely on top of the other two balls. "Are you okay?"

Warner nodded as he produced two loose buttons and a carrot out of his coat pocket. "I'm good. This has been fun. I was thinking how we needed this fun in our lives."

He let Lizzy do the honors of creating a face for the snowman. When the character was complete, including stick arms, the three of them stood back to survey their work.

"What did one snowman say to the other?" Star asked Lizzy.

"I don't know."

"Do you smell carrots?"

Lizzy giggled.

Star's smile faded into a frown as she scrutinized their creation. "No, I don't think I'm any kind of artist."

"No, but that gives me an idea," Warner said. "We can do different activities throughout the day and see if any of them jog your memory."

"I'd like that." Star packed a small snowball. "Starting with a snowball fight."

She handed the snowball to Lizzy who took the cue and hurled it at her father. He gaped in pretend shock as it splattered harmlessly against his coat. Lizzy's delightful laughter filled the air.

"Run for cover!" Star shouted with a mischievous grin.

Lizzy followed her behind a large tree trunk. Bandit ran with them, bounding through the snow.

"Where is the loyalty to family?" Warner asked his daughter with playful incredulity.

"Take no prisoners!" Star cried.

They volleyed snowballs back-and-forth, two against one, with Star mostly feeding snowballs to Lizzy. In the end, Warner launched an offensive attack. When he got close to Lizzy, he picked her up and spun in a circle as she giggled.

"You're covered in snow!" she cried.

"Thanks to you!" he said.

He looked at Star and realized she'd somehow managed to dodge all the snowballs. She'd dashed through the snow, light on her feet, rolled and ducked without ever having taken a hit.

Now, after robust activity, she looked angelic with rosy cheeks surrounded by dark hair framed in a snowy landscape. She picked up Bandit and cradled the puppy.

"Maybe you're an acrobat," he suggested to Star as he sat Lizzy back down on the ground.

He brushed snow out of his hair as he shivered. "I think snow got inside my coat. Let's get inside, warm up, and have a little hot chocolate."

"Hot chocolate!" Lizzy beamed.

AFTER HOT CHOCOLATE, Lizzy and Star sculpted the solar system out of Playdough while Warner and his mom prepared Christmas dinner.

"Definitely not a sculptor," Star said, surveying her lumpy planets.

Warner grinned when he looked up from his turkey basting.

She ran a finger along a few calluses on her hands. Their appearance suggested she wasn't averse to getting her hands dirty but not so much that manual labor constituted her livelihood. Her nails were trimmed short.

The snowball fight had felt like she was in her element. She was agile and could predict people's intentions from slight shifts in weight and body language.

After her shower earlier, she had looked over her body for evidence of the past that might trigger her memory. She'd had some type of orthoscopic knee surgery. As for her age, she guessed she was about thirty. Her abdomen was smooth and flat—indicative of good fitness, and no sign of stretch marks.

She glanced at Lizzy molding the Playdough. Did the other woman want children? Did her fiancé?

"Do you remember *anything*?" the child said, rolling out yellow Playdough for Saturn's rings.

Star picked up a handful of yellow Playdough and massaged it with her fingers. "I woke up in the cold snow in the dark of night with Bandit tucked in my jacket." Star began the story in a tone more like a tale than the truth, since the experience seemed fanciful. "Then, I saw a bright star. Except, this star wasn't high in the sky. It hung just over the horizon of the trees and then dropped into the forest. So, I followed it here, to this cabin."

The glowing light she'd seen had gone so far as to illuminate the correct numbers on the key code so she could let herself inside the cabin. She decided to omit that part since it seemed too surreal. "I was so exhausted that I plopped on the couch and slept."

Lizzy beamed at her with a wide smile and large brown eyes. "Wow! Gramma, did you hear that?"

Louise chuckled. "I sure did." She was mixing stuffing in a large bowl.

Warner stared at Star in shock.

"Did I say something wrong?" Star asked.

Louise reached over and closed Warner's mouth with a finger under his jaw. "Not at all, dear. We have a long history with the Christmas Star."

"What do you mean?" Star set the Playdough down.

Warner averted his gaze as he busied himself mixing mashed potatoes with intense vigor.

Louise explained, "Every year, someone in the Orion family reports seeing a star—unexplained by constellations or planets. It may be in the sky or on earth or even more of a light than a star. But it always precedes a miracle."

"Or directly causes one," Ralph interjected, planting a kiss on his wife's cheek.

"Yes. Ralph was walking downtown, and a bright star in a window caught his attention—too bright to be a light on the inside and not the right angle to be the sun reflecting off something. Anyway, he hesitated crossing the road and avoided getting hit by a truck running the traffic light."

"That must have been scary," Star said.

"We've come to believe the star is our Christmas Spirit looking out for us," Louise said.

"Does it always save lives?" Star asked, thinking about

how the star she'd seen had saved her life by leading her to the cabin.

"No. Sometimes it presents opportunity. Sometimes it gives strength," Louise said.

"How so?"

"It gave our niece strength one year when she was desolate about her overseas tour. She's out of the Marines now, but those were tough times," Ralph said, washing mixing bowls and measuring cups.

Star smiled. "I love your Christmas Star story. And maybe it led me here because it knew your family would be so kind while I get my memories back."

"Daddy says the star *is* love but doesn't *give* love." Lizzy put a speck of Playdough on the largest planet to represent Jupiter's red spot.

"What does he mean by that?" Star asked.

She poked at the planet without looking up. "I told him I wanted a new mom, and he said the star doesn't work that way. That's why I said you must be from Santa."

"Oh."

A new mom? Which meant a new wife for Warner. She glanced in his direction, but he was stirring something in a small pot—possibly gravy—on the stove, as if creating a culinary masterpiece. The conversation about the Christmas Star and Lizzy's wish seemed to make him uncomfortable. And here was Star, feeding into Lizzy's dreams and complicating his situation.

"Lizzy, you and you father are wonderful people. The right new mom will come along when it's time. I wouldn't worry about that."

The room fell silent as Star rolled the tiniest ball of black Playdough to represent Pluto.

235

CHAPTER 5

Over dinner, Warner and his parents told Star about their ski trip to Wintergreen last year and their plans to go again in February. Lizzy talked animatedly about her first time skiing and riding the lifts. He enjoyed her enthusiasm, as it gave him the feeling he was succeeding as a single father.

"Daddy's really good. He can ski backwards like the ski instructor. And he can do the black slopes. I have to practice more to get to blue first."

When they finished the meal and Warner began clearing the table, Star jumped to help. He started washing as she brought plates and platters to him.

Louise took Lizzy upstairs for her evening bath as Ralph plopped into the living room recliner with his iPad in hand.

"Ever been skiing?" Warner asked her, needing the conversation to keep his thoughts platonic as he learned more about her.

She shook her head. "Not sure. It's not conjuring

images. I feel like I would enjoy it, if that makes sense. The rush of speed, the wind in my hair."

"You think you have a daredevil side?"

"Adventurous." She grinned, handing him an empty platter.

She hadn't spoken the word in a flirtatious manner, but rather matter-of-factly. Still, Warner briefly entertained what it might be like to explore her adventurous side, before squelching those thoughts.

"Hopefully not the type of adventure these yahoos are taking," Ralph interjected as he thumped his fingers against his iPad screen.

"What's that, Dad?"

"These escaped convicts. The Grinch Brothers."

"Yeah, I saw them on the news yesterday."

"Well, they won't get anywhere today with the snow and ice."

The weather also kept Star under Warner's roof, but fortunately they had an unused bedroom so she wouldn't have to crash on the couch again. But their time had an expiration date—a much needed one, he reminded himself—since she had her own family to return to.

AFTER THE DISHES WERE DONE, Warner tucked Lizzy into bed. His daughter had carried Bandit with her, but he seemed to be looking around for his owner.

"He belongs to Star, sweetie." He didn't need Lizzy sleeping with the dog and bonding that much more.

"Today was best Christmas ever."

He chuckled. "I'm glad you had fun." He tucked the covers around her.

"Can Star stay? Sometimes you talk about her leaving, but I don't want to give her back. She's our present from Santa."

"She has to go back to her family. I'm sure they miss her."

"But she doesn't have a family."

"Everyone has a family. She doesn't remember them right now, but she will."

"Don't send Star away."

"I—" He hung his head. There was no winning this battle, and Lizzy's worry suggested he would be the one to take the blame when Star had to leave.

"Let's read one of the books we brought from home." He read *Where the Wild Things Are,* and Lizzy thankfully relaxed into the story.

After kissing her forehead and bidding goodnight, he went back downstairs and put sheets on the bed in the extra room so Star would have a place to sleep. When he went back into the living room, he scanned the area for Star.

"Outside," his father said from the recliner as he scrolled through his electronic notebook.

"Was I that obvious?"

Ralph shrugged without looking up.

Warner bundled up and stepped onto the back porch where Star was gazing up at a crescent moon. The sky was clear now, though another snowfall was expected in the early morning.

"Can I join you?" he asked her.

"Certainly."

He closed the sliding glass door behind him.

"I'm sure I've stared at the sky a hundred times in my lifetime, but tonight it feels magical," she said.

"I never get tired of stargazing." But he didn't look up at them. He was admiring the silhouette of her face, committing it to memory for when—in the words of Lizzy—he sent Star away.

He tore his gaze from her to look at the sky. "You see those two brighter stars? Those are the heads of the Gemini twins. If you follow them down and connect the dots, you'll see two stick figures holding hands. One head —the brightest—is Castor, a star system fifty-two light years from earth. The other head, Pollux, is a giant star with an extrasolar planet revolving around it."

"It's amazing." She craned her head back as she star-gazed, and Warner glimpsed the soft, pale skin of her neck.

She shook her head. "I don't know about twins, though. They look nothing alike. Castor's head is bigger, and his legs are longer."

Warner laughed. "Agreed. In Greek mythology, they are actually not twins. Over there is the Orion constella-tion. You can find it by the three stars in alignment repre-senting the hunter's belt."

"Hunter?"

"In Greek mythology, Orion was a supernaturally strong giant and hunter. When he threatened to kill every creature on earth, Gaia set a scorpion on him."

"Kudos to Mother Earth."

"And that's why you won't see Orion and Scorpius in the sky at the same time."

She turned to look at him. "Fascinating. I guess you learn a lot of Greek mythology in astronomy."

"Greek, Middle East, European. It is fascinating. Humankind has been staring at the same sky for millions of years and making up stories about the stars."

She shivered. "I think if it wasn't so cold, I could lay on a deck chair and stare up for hours. Goodnight, Warner. And thank you again for today."

He remained on the deck as she went back inside the cabin. He had only convinced his wife to stargaze a few times before they married. It seemed life had grown busy after that, and they hadn't made the effort to stay connected. If they hadn't taken their time together for granted and had known it would be so brief, he liked to think they would have enjoyed more moments like this. Perhaps.

If he ever did find love again, he was going to savor it until the end.

Star crawled into bed, joined by Bandit. When he nestled into her hair, she had a feeling he was accustomed to this routine. She wished she could remember. And yet her day had been so blissful, she wondered how it compared to her regular life.

Was there a reason she couldn't remember who she was? Was there something she psychologically wanted to leave behind, as Ralph had alluded to?

She felt the ring on her finger and momentarily felt sad to think there might be someone out there whose love she was missing, and vice versa. Was the man to whom she was engaged half the man Warner was? But a comparison wasn't fair to her mystery fiancé. She had a history with that man, while she'd only known Warner for a day. A day of carefree fun and lingering stares. She'd meant what she said about stargazing for hours but hadn't added that she would enjoy it more if he was beside her describing the constellations and the stories written about them in his deep, soothing voice. How ridiculous was she to be drawn to a man she'd only just met?

But it wasn't just Warner. His entire family had enchanted her. Was she this fanciful in her real life? Or had she been entranced by the magic of the holiday season? What if she came face-to-face with her fiancé and didn't want that life anymore?

No. Something would trigger her memory, and she would go back to being the person she was. Perhaps she could stay friends with Warner, gentleman and family man. How many families would have been so accommodating on Christmas day to a stranger dropping in abruptly and unannounced?

She rubbed around Bandit's ears, which seemed to calm her as much as it did the dog. Time. Time and patience would restore her memories.

She couldn't stay in a fantasy of Christmas every day and insert herself into Lizzy's life. Her presence seemed unfair to the child. Star had seen Warner's mixed emotions throughout the day—enjoyment of how smitten Lizzy was with her and turmoil at what the child would go through when she left, especially since Lizzy thought she was her special Santa delivery.

Star slipped into sleep, imagining she would dream of sugar plums and snowball fights, but something darker invaded her mind.

She found herself dressed in black combat fatigues with a knife strapped to one thigh. She looked down at the weapon she was holding—an AK-47. How did she know the name of the monstrosity in her hands?

She glanced at two other men around her, also in black fatigues with the same automatic weapons. Their faces looked hard and battle ready.

"Hey Mad-eye, which one do you want to take for interrogation?" one of the men asked her.

Mad-eye? No. Something was very wrong here. She looked at the people the man had gestured toward.

Five individuals knelt on the dirt with black masks over their heads. Their hands were secured behind their back with twist ties. They wore civilian clothing––blue jeans and khaki pants. From the parts of their bodies she could see, they were all Caucasian, some men and some women.

"The one in the middle," she heard herself say in a voice more rigid than she'd used at any point during Christmas day.

What?! No, no, no. This was all wrong. She was holding unarmed hostages at gunpoint. What kind of maniac was she?

One man swung the AK-47 over his shoulder and around his back where the strap held it in place. He then grabbed the hostage in the middle, a woman, up by the ponytail beneath her hood. She gasped and struggled to her feet. He roughly led her away with a thick, meaty hand on the captive's forearm.

Star jolted up in bed, panting. She tried to shake the scene from her mind even as the sensation of holding cold, deadly steel in her fingertips lingered.

It had been only a dream. Nightmares happened all the time, and that didn't make them real. But it felt real. Cold sweat trickled down her neck. The scene she'd just witnessed felt like a memory.

Adventurous, she'd told Warner. But perhaps she should have said *dangerous*.

Heart still thudding, she left Bandit sleeping in the bed and went to the kitchen for a glass of water.

WARNER HAD WOKEN at four a.m. and been unable to fall back to sleep. He worked on his laptop in bed, but then searched the Internet for information on amnesia.

The details he found suggested the problem was as his father mentioned—triggered by a combination of trauma and also emotional stress. But either could cause amnesia without the other. Warner wondered what emotional distress such a lovely, personable woman might have experienced that could have contributed to memory loss.

He also learned that memory loss didn't wipe one's personality, meaning that the humorous, engaging Star he knew was the same type of person prior to arriving on his couch—though perhaps unburdened by what had been troubling her.

He wondered if it had something to do with her engagement. Every time she looked at her ring, her brow furrowed. He would have expected the sight of it and all it represented to cause a smile.

His ears perked up at the sound of noise coming from downstairs. Lizzy? She rarely got up in the night, but she'd had quite an exciting day—what with Santa's supposed gift. He thought he'd better go down and check.

He arrived in the kitchen to see Star set a glass of water down and lean heavily on the counter, dropping her head to her chin.

"Are you okay?" he asked.

She took a shaky breath. "Bad dream."

She wore a flannel pajama shirt that covered down to her mid-thigh. He hadn't realized his mother had swiped one of his shirts for Star, but never had the garment looked so good.

"Can I get you anything?"

She looked up at him through those long lashes and with those big blue eyes, deep enough to drown in. He couldn't afford to dive into that place. He swallowed hard and stood frozen.

She rolled her neck in a slow circle. "Do you think I could've been a bad person in my other life?"

"No," he said without hesitation. He gave a nervous chuckle. More firmly he said, "I wouldn't believe that for a second. You have a good heart."

"I hope you're right."

"Do you want to talk about the dream?"

"No."

Against his better judgment for what this was going to

do to *his* heart in the near future, he stepped toward Star and took her into his arms.

She didn't shed a tear, but she did relax into him. Her fingers curled the back of his pajama shirt into tight little balls, as if she was squeezing the tension out of herself and into those concentrated spots.

He smelled the scent of vanilla in her hair and had the audacity to observe how nicely their bodies fit together.

He gave her one last, purely platonic squeeze before pulling away and turning toward the coffeemaker. "Let's get some caffeine started." He hoped she didn't notice the huskiness in his voice.

"Thank you, Warner."

He cleared his throat. "We'll do more activities today and see if any of your memories surface."

CHAPTER 6

Star diced tomatoes, mushrooms, green peppers, and onions while Warner cooked Italian sausage on a cast-iron skillet. Lizzy played on the floor with Bandit and a small stick Warner had given her. She laughed and squealed as he chased her and climbed all over her. Star watched, amused, but also ready to intervene if the puppy played too rough for a six-year-old.

Because her clothes had been washed, Star was back in her comfy jeans and sweater. She had spent the morning walking outside and trying to remember her past.

The scent of fresh vegetables filled the kitchen. For a few moments, as Star held the large knife and methodically chopped, she thought about her nightmare and the knife that had been strapped to her thigh.

Ontario ASEK-AircrewTM Survival Egress knife.

Her blood chilled at the thought of what her former life consisted of that she would know different types of weapons. In fact, in her mind's eye, she could picture different knives and their names.

"How's it going over there?" Warner asked. "Any sudden sensations, like you might be an award-winning chef?"

She let out a nervous chuckle and shelved further thoughts about types of weapons. "No. No chef, but something about the weight of the knife feels familiar. Maybe I'm a carny. A knife thrower in a circus."

Warner arched a playful eyebrow.

Star spun the handle of the kitchen knife in the palm of her hand followed by the flick of her wrist into the air for a triple flip before she caught the handle again.

"Wow! That was cool!" Lizzy said.

Star smiled at her newly discovered talent before faltering when she caught the nervous look in Warner's eyes. She dropped her head and resumed chopping onions as he added the sausage to the spaghetti sauce.

She moved on to spreading garlic butter onto the Italian bread while Warner cooked noodles. His parents and Lizzy set to work setting the table.

OVER LUNCH, Star learned that Warner's parents were retired. His father was a former political science teacher, and his mother had taught high school algebra.

As she twirled noodles and sauce onto her fork, she observed how she hadn't forgotten how to eat spaghetti.

"What about you, Lizzy? What are you going to be when you grow up?" She wondered if the girl would carry on the teaching tradition.

"I want to be an astronaut."

"With an astronomer as a father, you probably know all about space, planets, and the galaxies. An astronaut sounds exciting." During their Playdough sculpting, Lizzy had sized the planets to scale and lined them up accurately.

"What are you going to do if your memories don't come back?" the girl asked her.

"When the snow is cleared up, I should be able to find my car again, or truck, or whatever I drive. Hopefully, I'll find my purse with identification or vehicle registration. Once I have that information, I'll be able to reconnect with my family and re-discover who I am." She made it sound simple and cheery, but so many 'ifs' lurked in there —*if* she had a car, *if* she found her car, *if* she had family, and *if* seeing them triggered the return of her memories. She at least had a fiancé somewhere.

"Lizzy, are there any games you want to play?" Louise asked, changing the subject.

"Yeah!"

Louise stood and began clearing the table. "The other day, I noticed the owners keep games in the cabinet over there. Why don't you dig in and see what looks fun? You, Star, and your dad can play on the coffee table."

Lizzy bounded out of her chair to pick out a game.

"I can help," Star said, picking up her plate to clear the table.

"You are helping." Louise nodded in Lizzy's direction as she took the plate from Star.

Star followed Warner over to the coffee table in the living room as Lizzy pulled out *Operation*. They formed a circle, sitting cross-legged on the carpet. Bandit crawled into her lap and rested his head on her knee. Star helped them put the plastic "body parts" in the man and check the functionality of the game.

A few minutes into the game, Star was winning.

"Those are some steady hands," Warner said.

She'd relaxed after the big meal to enjoy the moment with father and daughter but hadn't intended to win—did she have a competitive side, too?

"Maybe I'm a surgeon." She grinned, but it faded quickly. What if she was marrying a surgeon? She didn't think she would enjoy a relationship with someone who worked long hours. Unless, of course, she worked long hours, too.

Ralph peered over to survey her work. "Fine motor skills. Maybe you make jewelry."

"Artistic painter," Louise suggested from the kitchen sink.

Star used the tweezers to reach for the butterfly in the upper abdomen. But what organ was actually there? A little to the left—the man's right—would be the liver. To the right—the man's left—would be the stomach. Between those was the xiphoid process. Thrusting a sharp weapon upward and under the xiphoid would puncture the heart.

How… no, *why* did she know that?

Her hand shook—setting off the electric buzzer—and she dropped the plastic butterfly.

"You okay?" Warner asked.

Without making eye contact, she passed off the tweezers. "Yeah, your turn."

❄

WHEN THEY FINISHED THE GAME, Bandit found his way into Warner's lap. He chuckled and petted the playful puppy. His hair felt soft, like a cashmere sweater with a mix of black, brown, white, and russet colors. He tried to gauge how old the dog might be. Maybe six months? He was some type of gorgeous husky hybrid, but the breed he'd been mixed with would make him smaller than a standard husky when full grown, probably more manageable for a six-year-old girl.

Whoa.

He was definitely not thinking about a puppy for Lizzy. He continued to pet the dog, who advanced into his lap and climbed higher and higher, trying to reach to lick his face. Up close, Warner got a good look at the dog's eyes. The irises reminded him of Star's eyes—a kaleidoscope of blue and silver.

He still puzzled over how the woman had arrived at his cabin and wondered what the connection was to some of her ongoing strange behavior. She had a good sense of humor and warm smile, but moments appeared when she grew a little more guarded. He wondered if she'd glimpsed her past and found it unpleasant.

He wished she would open up to him, and maybe they could explore whatever pieces she was remembering together. But they hardly knew each other. Why would she open up to him?

Bandit nipped at his hand and then drew back slightly, as if knowing he'd done something he wasn't supposed to. Warner scratched around his ears to let him know all was forgiven. Who wouldn't forgive a face like that?

Maybe when Star left, he could buy himself and Lizzy

a consolation prize in the form of a new puppy. It wouldn't be this one, but it would be something.

IN THE LATE AFTERNOON, they sat around the fire reading books. Warner read a Dan Brown novel, Star had picked up *The Girl with the Dragon Tattoo*, Ralph flipped through *A Christmas Carol*, and Louise read Shel Silverstein poems to Lizzy.

"I'm going to grab some firewood." Warner carried his boots from the front door to the back where a large porch overlooked the snowy mountainside. He'd discovered on their first day that the firewood was stored beneath the porch, which wrapped around the side and back of the cabin.

Star stood and set aside her book. "I'll help. I could use a leg stretch."

He'd noticed that if someone else was working, Star couldn't be idle. She was helpful by nature—an attribute he admired.

After they bundled in coats and boots, they ventured onto the back porch. Light snow fell from a gray, dusky sky. Dark tree branches carried a layer of powder on top. Deep green pine needles protruded from the cone-shaped snow covering the pine trees.

Star gasped. "It's beautiful out here."

"Yes, it is." But he wasn't looking at the mountain view.

When she noticed his stare, her cheeks flushed. Warner pulled his gaze away from her lovely face and turned abruptly. He started down the stairs, silently scolding himself for his behavior—again.

Several inches of snow layered each step. He needed to scrape those clear before carrying the wood back up. A few steps from the bottom, the trek turned slippery as the snow, now packed into the soles of his boots, obliterated the tread on the bottom.

He held onto the rail, but felt his footing go, and he pitched forward.

A hand clamped over his coat, steadying him.

"Gotcha."

"Thanks. Those are some quick reflexes," he said, noting she was strong, too.

When she let go, he carefully reached the bottom of the stairs. He turned and extended a hand to help her down, but when she went to take his hand, her footing slipped.

He moved to catch her elbow and keep her from falling, but his sudden motion made him slip backward and pull her with him. He landed in the soft snow as she landed on top of him.

He stared in stunned silence at how close her lips were to his. Her dark hair fell around her, spilling onto him.

"I'm sorry." Her voice sounded breathless.

"It's my fault." He reached up and tucked a strand of hair behind her ear. "I'm sorry."

Her head lowered slightly and stopped, making a kiss an entirely too easy undertaking. "Warner."

"Don't," he said firmly, shattering any possibility of intimacy. He shifted his weight. "I'll help you up."

They pushed to their feet and brushed off the snow.

Warner didn't know what Star intended to say, but any of it would have been wrong. He didn't want any words expressing an attraction they couldn't explore. He didn't want an apology for circumstances out of her control. She was here alone, and yet unavailable. Those were the only facts he needed to accept.

He grabbed the shovel next to the woodpile and began clearing the snow from the stairs.

Star filled her arms with chopped wood and silently walked past him up the stairs, onto the porch, and back into the house.

STAR CAME BACK DOWN for another load of wood and passed Warner as he scraped the stairs with a small dirt shovel while avoiding eye contact with her.

She'd screwed up that moment. The man had the decency to let her stay under his roof and eat his food, and she had the audacity to contemplate kissing him. She was lucky all he did was give her a command—"don't"—rather than send her packing.

Was the phrase still *"send her packing"* if she had nothing to pack?

She walked past an axe and rake propped against one wall, as the shovel had been before Warner put it to use. After loading more logs into her arms, she headed for the stairs. She briefly considered walking up the slope on the side of the house to the front door to avoid traipsing through Warner's snow removal project, but the way appeared just steep enough she might need her hands free to help with balance. She chose the stairs and walked up with the logs as unobtrusively as she could.

Was this the type of woman she was—literally falling over the first man she met? Not only was she engaged and filled with dangerous knowledge about how to mortally wound someone, she had held hostages at gunpoint. She did not need to bring her sordid past—or present—into this man's peaceful life with his family.

After dropping off the wood, she went out front and rechecked the roads. Not safe yet. She borrowed Louise's phone and called the police, but still no one had reported a missing woman.

She needed only to keep her hands—and mouth—to herself until the roads cleared. In the meantime, she'd be sure to earn her keep.

CHAPTER 7

After dinner, they played Scrabble, and Louise beat everyone in the word game. Star enjoyed the family banter, red wine, and faint Christmas music playing in the background.

Louise stood. "Lizzy, hon, let's get bath and bedtime going."

Warner started to stand. "I'll take care of it, Mom."

She waved a hand at him. "Nonsense, you've got company. Say goodnight, Lizzy."

Reluctantly, Lizzy stood from her toys still around the tree and went to her father. "Night, Dad."

He gave her a long, lingering hug. "Goodnight, Sweetheart."

To Star's surprise, Lizzy came to her next and stepped right into her, wrapping small arms around her neck. "Night, Star."

Star returned the embrace, feeling her small body, and shocked at the way her own heart swelled at the gesture.

"Goodnight, Lizzy. I had so much fun with you today."

"Me, too." The girl pulled away and looked up at her. "Best Christmas ever." She bent down and patted Bandit who was gnawing on a stick beside Star.

A lumped caused Star's throat to close beyond the ability to speak. Tears welled briefly in her eyes, but she blinked them away. Surely, if she was some hardened killer, a six-year-old couldn't bring her to tears.

"Do you want to try chess next?" Warner asked Star as they shoveled letters back into the Scrabble box.

"Sure."

Ralph moved to sit in the recliner, thumbing through his iPad. "Police are still hunting for the Grinch brothers."

Star set up the pieces on the chessboard. "Beg your pardon?" She remembered he'd mentioned them last night as well.

Warner moved a bishop. "They're actually the Green brothers, and they broke out of jail. The news is calling them the *Grinch Brothers* because they escaped on Christmas Eve."

Ralph added, "They were spotted driving a red pickup, high-tailing it west. They ought to be clean through to Tennessee by now, unless they're stuck somewhere due to the inclement weather."

A sharp pain hit Star's left temple and streaked behind her eye. She pressed her palm to her orbit, and the pain passed as quickly as it had come.

"Are you okay?" Warner asked.

"Just tired."

"We don't have to play."

"No, no. I want to play."

Forty-five minutes later, Warner tipped his king over

and accepted defeat humbly. "Well done. Perhaps you have a career involving strategy. Congratulations."

"I'm not sure that narrows it down, but I'll admit it feels nice to succeed at something today," Star said, repositioning the game pieces.

Louise returned from tucking Lizzy into bed. She walked over to the stereo and turned up the volume on the Christmas music.

"May I have this dance?" she asked Ralph.

"Of course." He rose from his chair, set down the iPad, and took her in his arms.

They danced and swayed to "Jingle Bell Rock."

Star watched them, wondering what the security of a long-term relationship like that would feel like. So far, she had a mystery fiancé who still hadn't reported her missing.

Warner extended a hand toward her. "Care to dance?"

She took the hand, and he pulled her up. "I don't know if I know how."

"You could be a seasoned ballroom dancer. Only one way to find out."

She laughed as he twirled her. She discovered she had the rhythm to dance and felt like butter in his hands, moving and turning to the slightest pressure from his fingertips. At the end of the song, he took her into a low dip. She laughed as he up righted her in his arms.

Silent Night began playing.

They froze in each other's arms, unsure if a slow dance was a good idea.

The room felt suddenly hot. Star looked over to see Warner's parents observing the pair of them with inquisitive stares. Star and Warner simultaneously stepped back from each other, their arms falling to their sides.

"I should go to bed," she stammered.

She bid everyone good night and took Bandit outside —partly to let him take care of business before calling it a night and partly to let the frigid air cool her fervor.

She wanted to stick her head in the snow like an ostrich. Did such chemistry really flare between two people who'd only known each other two days? Warner set her core alight with his dark, dancing eyes, making her feel like a star about to burst.

Maybe this was a side effect of amnesia—wanting to emotionally latch on to the first person she saw. Except, she was no imprinting baby duck. She was a hot-blooded woman. But she was also a rational adult who wouldn't succumb to impulse. She wasn't right for Warner and Lizzy, although surely some sort of hardened, gun-toting killer wouldn't be flustered and feverish in the arms of a man.

Nothing made sense in her life, and drawing Warner into the disarray was unfair.

WARNER STOOD speechless as Star disappeared. What had he been thinking, asking her to dance? She'd had such longing in her eyes watching his parents dance that he'd wanted to erase her sadness. And, *stars above*, he'd wanted to kiss her. What kind of man made a move on an engaged woman?

He ran a hand through his hair and realized his

parents were still watching him. At least Lizzy hadn't been around to see her father's ridiculous behavior. He didn't want to send her mixed messages about a woman who'd soon be out of their lives.

"I think I've lost my mind," he told them.

"For being attracted to a beautiful woman?" his mom asked gently.

He looked at the pair of them arm in arm. He wanted what they had. "First woman to come along since Tina's death, and I'm throwing myself at her."

"Not the first," his father pointed out.

Warner couldn't argue that point. He'd had a few opportunities but had let them fizzle.

"That wasn't throwing yourself at her," his mother said.

"She's been here less than two days. And she's engaged."

"There's a reason she's here," Louise said. "Even if we don't yet know why."

"Are you implying she's our Christmas miracle?"

"She did say a star brought her here."

He puffed out his cheeks and blew out a slow exhale. He wanted to believe in their family tradition of the Christmas Star, but it didn't extend to relationships as far as he knew. And if he allowed himself to become any more attached to Star, his heart would be shredded that much more when she had to return to her family.

He'd glimpsed the fire in her eyes several times, and those moments thrilled him more than they should have. Her attraction to him flattered him and fueled his desires to touch her. His actions weren't fair to her, probably making her feel unfaithful to her future husband.

STAR WOKE WITH A START.

Memories, or another nightmare?

Images of violence flashed before her eyes. She'd been somewhere with dry air and brittle dirt. She hunkered behind a stone half-wall with a dozen other men and women. They were taking enemy fire, but they were also returning it.

She'd been shooting at people. What kind of monster was she?

The kind that didn't need to be around a peaceful family in an isolated cabin. She rolled out of bed and dressed. Was she a danger to them? She refused to be responsible for bringing violence into their lives.

She glanced at the bedside clock: 5:30 A.M. She hadn't heard anyone in the Orion family stirring and decided she needed to leave before one of them saw her. She didn't want to explain an abrupt departure, because that would involve describing her dreams. And then they would learn what type of person she really was.

She folded Warner's flannel night shirt and left in on top of the bed, resisting the juvenile urge to take something of his with her.

After she entered the kitchen, she found a blank piece of paper and pen and left a note.

She grabbed a bottle of water and a container of lunchmeat from the fridge to make sure she had Bandit taken care of in case the walk proved long. She promised herself she'd find the Orion family later and pay them back for everything. After pulling on her coat, hat, and gloves, she tucked the puppy and the perishables inside her coat before slipping on her boots.

She stepped out of the door, quietly closing it behind her. The gray morning was cold, but a brisk pace would keep her warm. Her boots crunched on the snow as she walked to the end of the driveway. With relief, she noted the road now looked passable.

She walked along the highway as close to the piled mounds of snow as she could as she tried to make sense of the pieces of a life she couldn't remember or reassemble.

Hostages.

Mad-eye.

Engaged.

Bits of memories continued to pepper her mind as if someone chucked puzzle pieces at her with no cover image for reference.

"Oh, I wish you had found a man instead of a dog."

Whose voice was that? A woman. Older. Maybe sixties.

"Uh-huh. You sure you're not up to some secret spy mission?" Another familiar voice, but this one was male and younger. His tone sounded teasing, playful.

"We're under attack! We need an extraction!" A harsh, commanding voice screamed.

WARNER DRESSED and headed downstairs filled with a mixture of excitement and dread. He quite enjoyed seeing Star first thing in the morning, but she wasn't his to keep. And why should he want to? He'd only known her two days. And she was engaged.

Today, the roads would be cleared, and they would continue the hunt for her identity. This time beyond the confines of the cabin. He would try the police department and missing person's registries again. Surely by now her fiancé would have reported her missing.

When he reached the kitchen, the lack of light and prepared coffee told him she wasn't awake yet. Maybe she was sleeping well this time. He turned on the light and started the brewer, admittedly not as stealthily as he could have been, in hopes of waking her and having the first few quiet moments of daylight to share with her.

He spotted a note addressed to him.

No.

His heart ached and started to drip, drip, drip like a leaky faucet. How had he let himself get so attached to someone he barely knew?

Dear Warner,

I'm off in search of memories. I've intruded on your family's holiday long enough. I'm eternally grateful for the hospitality you've shown me.

—Star

He reread the note and even turned it over, as if looking for more. Her written words made no promise to return to him. But of course she couldn't make that promise without knowing what type of environment she would enter to when her memories reappeared.

Guilt gnawed at the frayed edges of his emotions. The last thing he'd done with her was dance. Perhaps his actions drove her to leave without a personable goodbye.

Now, he'd have to tell Lizzy that Star had left. He'd been dreading the inevitable moment ever since his daughter had bounded down the stairs claiming Star was her Christmas wish come true.

CHAPTER 8

Star snapped out of her daydream when a red truck driving too fast almost clipped her with the side-view mirror. It never slowed, as though the driver and occupant hadn't registered a pedestrian walking on the side of the road—made narrow by the piled snow lining the edges.

At her current pace, she estimated she'd walked a few miles from the Orion's rented cabin. So far, no return of her memories and no abandoned vehicle. If she found her car or truck, she would surely find her ID.

A few minutes later, the next truck to approach drove more slowly and pulled to a stop beside her.

When the driver rolled down the window, he leaned over the passenger seat and smiled. He had a round face, thinning gray hair, and warm eyes encased in crow's feet.

"You all right, miss? Can I give you a ride somewhere?"

In the few seconds he took to pull over, roll down the window, and ask his question, Star's mind assessed for threats. She glimpsed the back of his truck—rope, sheers, tarp, and some lawn equipment.

She sensed he was genuine and posed no danger, but knew exactly what she'd do to defend herself if he displayed dark intentions. Was sizing up another person and whether she could physically best them part of normal human behavior or part of her shady past? Past or present?

"I actually lost my car somewhere off the road. I'm going to keep walking until I find it."

"I don't mind driving you up and down for a bit. I'd feel better trying to help rather than leave you on the side of a narrow road in the cold. Or I can call someone for you."

Bandit whined.

"I'll take that ride." She opened the door and climbed into the passenger seat. Warm air thawed her cold cheeks. "Thanks."

He began slowly driving as she looked out the window.

The news reported on the radio:

"Authorities report escaped convicts—Willie and Alvin Green—have been spotted in Patrick County. Although dubbed the Grinch Brothers for their holiday escape, police warn that the criminals are to be considered armed and dangerous."

The man turned off the radio. "I've been listening to this for the last several days. I guess it's part of the reason I didn't want you walking the road alone."

"I appreciate the assistance."

Bandit stuck his head out through her coat.

"Well, that's a cute fella."

"This is Bandit."

"I had an old hound used to follow me everywhere. Name was Pershing."

"Pershing? The World War I Army general?"

"I served in the army."

"Army. I was a special operations communication sergeant." A throbbing started in her left temple as memories flooded her mind. She'd been in the division that worked with communication gear and a range of specialized equipment, from encrypted satellite communications down to old style Morse key systems.

"Are you okay?"

"Yes." She took a breath to clear her thoughts and lifted a business card from the center console of the truck. "Is this you?"

Pole Davis, Tree Service

"Pole Davis at your service."

"Stella Maddox." The name flowed naturally off her tongue. She instantly remembered her Army nickname: Mad-eye.

"Still in the Army, Stella?"

"No. I did six years. I now train civilians on survival techniques."

Including staged kidnapping and hostage events, she remembered.

"Oh. There!" she spotted the top of her blue car.

He pulled over, turning on his hazard lights.

With the dog still in her coat, she got out of the car and looked over the embankment.

Pole walked around and stood beside her. He pulled on an Army baseball cap. "I've got a wench, but you're going to need quite the tow truck to pull you out." He withdrew his phone. "Need me to call?"

"Yes. Thank you." She was grateful for his hospitality and that he'd triggered her memories, unbeknownst to him.

She carefully picked her way down to her car, wanting to find her phone. It wouldn't have any charge left and might not work altogether after three days in the snow, but it was still like an appendage.

Now that talking to Pole had returned her memories, other flashes of her past were coming in rapid fire. After the Army, she'd earned a master's in education. She had tried teaching for a few years but wanted something unconventional, so she took a job with TSTS—Tactical Survival Training Specialists. She trained civilians in survival, especially with simulated events. The kidnapping and hostage trainees were usually people planning mission trips or job relocations into hostile territory and wanting to be prepared for worst-case scenarios.

She and her team carried unloaded props for the training. The only complaint they ever received from civilians was for not being harsh enough during the simulations.

Reaching her car, she felt giddy and free with the knowledge she wasn't the monster her nightmare had suggested. Those had been memories viewed out of context.

When she looked at the gnarled front of her car, pain shot through her forehead, momentarily blinding her as she remembered the car crash. A red truck had run her off the road. She recalled getting out of her car and taking the tumble. As she eased down the slope, she pictured the trajectory of her fall and where her phone might have gone. She let Bandit out into the snow as she dug.

"Are you okay?" Pole called down from the road.

"Yes. Just looking for my phone." Like a needle in a haystack, she thought.

A bright patch of snow caught her eye. Unnaturally bright. She looked up to the sky, but the light couldn't be explained by the sun or its reflection.

She clawed at the illuminated spot of snow. Three inches down, she found her phone. "Huh." The case still contained her license and credit card. She stuck it in her coat pocket with plans to charge the device later.

Standing and brushing snow off her knees, she thought of Warner and his family's Christmas Star. The star had shown her the way through the Christmas storm —a guiding light through cold and snow and darkness.

Then the red truck returned to the forefront of her mind. The red truck had hogged the road that night as it headed up the mountain, forcing her off of the edge. It had been the same red truck coming down the mountain today. Two men had been visible through the windshield.

Words replayed in her mind.

Two escaped convicts.

Red Chevy Colorado.

Grinch Brothers.

Spotted in Patrick County.

They had gone up the mountain and probably had to stop somewhere that night due to the weather. Now, with the roads clear, they were coming back down in the middle of an active manhunt for them. If they were listening to the radio or checking the news online, they would know they needed a new vehicle.

Stella sucked in a breath. "Lizzy. Warner."

The star hovering above the snow-covered ground shone brighter.

She thought of the red truck going fast down the mountain only thirty minutes ago. What were the odds of the Grinch Brothers stopping at the Orion's cabin?

But the news said authorities were closing in on them. If they were desperate for money or a new vehicle and saw the cabin lights from the road, it could lure them to the Orions. The family lit a fire every day, and smoke from the chimney would indicate it had warmth, food, and occupants who may have items of value to two men on the run—including a new vehicle. The driveway curved, which would make a good hiding place for a bright red truck.

"Are they in trouble?" Stella asked the light—the Christmas Spirit.

Blinking rapidly, the star shot up from the snow to eight feet off the ground.

-.--

She jolted at the flashing Morse code the star was emitting.

YES, it had answered.

Worry and fear for Warner and his family spiked her heart rate and sent blood rushing through her ears.

"Show me the way."

The star darted off through the trees. She scooped up Bandit and dashed through the snow, barely registering Pole calling to her.

"I'll be back!" she called to him, uncertain if he could hear her from the distance.

WARNER STARED AT THE FIRE, watching the flames dance rhythmically to an unheard beat.

Lizzy had taken the news of Star's departure hard. She blamed him for not believing the woman had been a gift —as if his negativity had driven her away. His daughter sulked alone in her room, angry with him.

His parents came to the sofa and sat on either side of him.

"Some Christmas Star," he complained. "What gift is given so briefly and taken so abruptly?" He understood she'd had to leave and wasn't angry at the woman, only frustrated with the circumstances.

He scrubbed his hands over his face as he leaned forward where he sat. "I liked her. A lot. More than I should have for someone engaged. More than what is rational for such a brief acquaintance."

His mom rubbed a hand along his back. "Maybe the gift wasn't the woman herself but the hope she brought."

"Hope?"

"Warner, since Tina's death, you've been thinking you

don't have it in you to form a romantic relationship. Now you know you can care for another woman."

He tried to let the wisdom of his mother's words sink in, but he still felt simultaneously hollow and critical of himself for having no justifiable cause to be so affected by Star's departure.

"Star is a good person," his father added. "She'll come back for a proper goodbye."

"I'm not sure goodbye will be any easier the second time around."

The front door burst open, and cold air flooded the cabin. Warner jumped to his feet and stopped at the sight of two hideous, snarling men in the doorway. He recognized the escaped convicts and instantly felt the danger they carried with them. With his heart thumping its way into his throat, he swallowed and took a protective stance in front of his parents.

Lizzy had gone to her room earlier. Would she stay up there and remain hidden until these criminals left? He'd give them whatever valuables he had—money, clothes, and the car—and hopefully that would be enough.

WHEN STELLA REACHED the Orion's rented cabin, acid threatened to burn a hole in her chest at the sight of a red truck parked off to one side, out of view of the road.

She circled the cabin, stealing glimpses of the inhabitants through the windows as she also caught her breath from the brisk hike here. Through a thin space between curtains, she could see the family huddled on the couch.

Safety existed in clustering the hostages, but it also gave the aggressors the advantage of keeping their victims contained.

Warner had a streak of blood down his temple that originated from a gash at his hairline. She wondered if he'd tried to resist or if the attackers stuck a blow as a demonstration that they weren't opposed to the use of force.

Grinch brother number one paced in front of the family on the couch, holding a poker stick. He had dark hair framing a pock-marked face. He wore jeans and a grease-stained shirt—at least, she hoped it was grease and not something belonging to his last victim.

Grinch brother number two was rummaging through the main level bedroom—the one Louise and Ralph had been staying in. She didn't see Lizzy, though she couldn't see into the upstairs rooms, only that the lights were on.

Stella weighed her options. She could monitor the situation. There was a chance the men would steal what they wanted and leave. Alternatively, she could take the offensive and have the advantage of a surprise attack. If she idly waited to see what two desperate men on the run from police known to incorporate violence into their thievery might do, one or more of the Orion's could be hurt before Stella intervened. Yet, if she attempted a rescue, she could cause an escalation in violence.

"Do they have guns?" she asked the Christmas Star in barely a whisper.

-. ---

No.

That was a relief.

The star dove along the slope of the mountain and around the back of the cabin. Well, she'd followed it this far; she might as well continue to trust the Orion Christmas spirit.

She climbed down the side and around to under the porch where the firewood was stored. A small ball in a purple coat sat on the ground.

"Lizzy?"

"Star!" She leapt up and into Stella's arms.

"Shhh. Are you okay?" She hugged the girl and stroked her blonde hair.

"Daddy said you were gone."

"I was gone, but your family's Christmas Star let me know I needed to come back. Can you see it?"

Lizzy wiped away tears and nodded as Stella set her down.

"Why are you outside in the cold?" She adjusted the girl's hat over her ears.

"I came outside to look for you. When I didn't find you, I stayed here and cried. Then I heard shouting."

"Does your dad know where you are?"

She shook her head with eyes downcast. She probably understood her father would be frantic if he discovered her missing.

"Lizzy, I have an important task for you. Are you up for it?"

She nodded.

Stella pulled Bandit out of her coat. "Can you look after my dog for me? Stay here with the star until I or your dad come back for you, okay?" She pulled out the food from her coat and set it on the woodpile.

Lizzy gathered the puppy in her arms and nodded. "You're not leaving?"

Stella pressed a gloved hand to the girl's cheek and gave her a tender smile. "I'm not leaving."

CHAPTER 9

arner watched their captors with clenched teeth. He didn't even register pain from the injury on his head. He registered anger. But he feared for his family, and any action he took could endanger them.

"Hurry up, Alvin!" the man with the crowbar shouted.

Warner couldn't take on a hardened escaped convict—much less one with a solid carbon steel crowbar for a weapon. When he'd told the pair of them to take whatever they wanted and leave, they'd replied with a blow to his head. He'd ducked just enough to take more of a glancing blow than a direct hit.

Better him than his parents, he thought. His father took blood thinners for an irregular heartbeat. Even a graze could be an emergency for him.

Warner listened to the sound of rummaging through the room. The one Grinch brother would be done with the main floor bedrooms and probably advance upstairs soon.

Upstairs to Lizzy.

She'd stayed hidden thus far. Maybe she would continue to do so.

"Is there a safe or something with valuables?" the one with the crowbar demanded.

"I don't know. We're renters," Warner answered, trying to keep his voice calm. "Take anything you want. The car keys are on the counter," he repeated.

On the counter beside his phone, he realized. But the Grinch Brothers could rob them and be gone before police arrived, even if he had access to his phone. If Warner was lucky, they'd take valuables and go.

He racked his brain for all the bits of news he'd heard —theft and violence. No reports had ever mentioned homicide. The thieves were making no effort to hide their identity from him and his parents, but that didn't mean they intended further harm. They were already wanted for escaping from prison, what was one more robbery charge in the mix? Perhaps this was wishful thinking on Warner's part.

The other brother emerged, hauling a suitcase in one hand and a knife he'd swiped from the kitchen in the other. "Mostly crap, but I grabbed a few things."

"Check upstairs."

Warner clenched his fists. If his family's Christmas Spirit planned to grant them a miracle this year, now was the time.

Alvin bounded up to the second floor as his watchful brother with the crowbar continued to pace.

He stopped abruptly, a slow, wicked smile curling his lips to reveal crooked, mostly metal teeth. His gaze flickered from the toy purple unicorn by the tree to the children's books to the Playdough near the fireplace.

His diabolic eyes slid toward Warner. "Where's the little girl?"

Over my dead body, Warner thought as every muscle in his body tensed for a fight.

Before violence could erupt, smoke poured out of the fireplace and filled the room. Warner turned and took his parents down to the floor to escape the fumes.

STELLA SNATCHED the shovel beside the woodpile and scurried back up the embankment toward the front of the house. She tucked the shovel into the back of her jacket with the handle sticking up before climbing the railing connected to one side of the house where the porch started.

"Hurry up, Alvin!" one man barked.

Fortunately, most of the railing was clear of snow and wouldn't be too slippery. After steadying herself, she took to the count of three before jumping and grasping the edge of the roof. She reached elbow high, and the snow kept her from making much noise. She threw a leg up onto the roof, knocking snow to the ground.

Although she did daily push-ups and planks, she had to use every ounce of upper body strength to pull herself onto the base of the eave. She swung one leg up. Her muscles shook and burned from the effort. Once she had a leg and arm up, she was able to get the rest of her body on the roof and she cleared the spot of snow.

Catching her breath, she slowly stood, careful to keep her balance.

The section of the roof where she stood had a gentle slope but soon became steeper as it peaked above the second-floor bedrooms. The snow would make the climb hazardous.

After venturing a few steps, she took out the shovel and tugged off her coat. She'd be cold again later, but for now—with the vigorous activity—she wouldn't miss it. She balanced the coat on the metal tip of the spade-shaped shovel and then stretched her arms and torso as far as she could and draped the jacket over the chimney crown, preventing the venting of smoke.

After tossing the shovel a ways off the roof, she let herself slide down the surface, facing the front yard. When she reached the edge, she flung herself toward one piles of snow Warner had banked while shoveling the driveway the other day. She had only seconds to hope this wasn't a bad idea when the side of her curled body hit the packed snow.

The impact jarred her body, and now she was half-covered in snow with no coat, but it had still been the fastest way down. If she'd tried to land feet first anywhere, the slippery surfaces could have proven hazardous.

Gritting her teeth through the discomfort, she rolled and pushed to her feet. She scrambled to the front door, where she crouched to one side and readied her shovel for her attack.

Panicked shouting emitted from inside the house.

❄

WARNER KEPT one arm over each of his parents as he held them unmoving on the ground near the couch. He needed to get them out of the house, but also needed to get Lizzy to safety.

Smoke poured out of the fireplace and rose to the ceiling, but soon the entire cabin would fill with deadly particles.

"What the—?" The man with the crowbar swatted uselessly at the thickening smoke.

"Is something on fire?" the other brother called down from the third floor.

"Alvin, let's get out of here!" He snatched the keys off the kitchen counter.

"I'm not finished, Willie," Alvin called out.

"Now!" He coughed and gagged. "I'll be in the car." Willie headed for the front door.

As he stepped outside, a thunk was followed by a grunt and a second thwack.

Star walked into the living room, leaving the front door open to vent the cabin. Her hair was a disheveled heap, and she was without her coat, with snow clinging to her sweater. She looked like some type of frost warrior. Was she wielding a shovel?

Behind her, Willie's feet were visible on the ground in a way suggesting he was face down. Smoke rolled out the open door, helping to clear the room.

She pressed a finger to her lips.

Warner nodded. Quiet. He didn't have a problem keeping silent so long as they got Lizzy out of the smoke infested upper level. But he hadn't called to her yet with the other criminal still up there.

Where is he? Star mouth.

Warner pointed upstairs.

She crept silently past him as eerily calm as a lion stalking a gazelle. He recalled how she'd flipped the kitchen knife so casually in her hand while chopping onions and how she dodged snowballs seemingly effortlessly.

Who was she?

As she passed him, she handed off the crowbar she'd apparently swiped from Willie while he was busy being unconscious.

She pointed her fingers from her eyes to the brother by the door. Warner understood. He was to watch Willie in case he tried to move.

He whispered to his parents. "Stay down."

Star positioned herself behind the stairs.

"Willie?" Alvin called, emerging from a room to lean over the railing. "Hey! What'd you do to Willie?" he shouted at Warner.

He guessed from Alvin's perspective, it looked like he'd been the one to take out his brother.

Alvin started downstairs, wielding the kitchen knife he'd grabbed earlier. The glint of metal looked as menacing as the snarl on his face.

Halfway down, Star thrust a hand through the stairs, catching Alvin by the ankle and sending him head first the rest of the way down.

The knife and bag he was carrying flew forward. In a quick motion, Star came around the stairs and struck

Alvin with the flat end of the shovel. He crumpled to the floor.

"Lizzy!" Warner shouted toward the stairs, wanting to run upstairs but not wanting to leave Star with two dangerous men, even though they were injured on the floor.

"She's safe," Star said. "Outside by the woodpile."

"How did you—? Who are you?" Warner stared at her. "Your memories?"

She smiled. "They all returned. My name is Stella Maddox."

"You came back."

"Your Christmas star alerted me you were in danger."

He wanted to reach for her, but they stood at opposite ends of the room, each guarding one brother.

Ralph came to stand by his side. "I'll watch him. You go check on Lizzy." He took the crowbar from his hand.

"I need to borrow someone's phone," Stella said.

Louise stood and walked to Stella, wrapping her arms around her. "Stella, our Christmas Star!"

Warner slipped on his boots and dashed outside. "Lizzy!?"

Stella used Louise's phone to call the police while plugging her own into one of their chargers. She told them their location and about the incident with the Grinch brothers. She also requested a fire truck since perhaps they could help clear the smoke infested cabin to make it habitable for the Orion's tonight.

Next, she dialed Pole's number from his business card she'd swiped. "It's Stella. I'm sorry for rushing out on you."

"Everything okay? The tow truck company has arrived and set to work."

"You remember those Grinch Brothers?"

"Yeah."

"They attacked the family I stayed with over Christmas. Everyone is okay, and the convicts are incapacitated for now. Would you be interested in bringing that rope from your truck bed in exchange for the reward money? I'd like to have them better restrained before the police arrive. They've been notified."

"You incapacitated them?"

She rolled her aching shoulder muscles. "Yeah, well. Army strong."

Pike chuckled. "I don't need a reward. I need to see your work first hand."

She gave him the cabin address, and he gave her the name and number of the tow truck company so she'd know how to track down her car after it was pulled off the tree.

While she'd been on the phone, Ralph found duct tape in the kitchen. He and Warner used the adhesive to bind the criminals' hands together.

Louise kept Lizzy outside, presumably so she wouldn't see the scary men cursing on the floor. Together, Louise and her granddaughter played in the snow with Bandit away from the house.

Stella climbed the roof again and retrieved her coat. With the adrenaline ebbing, she was getting cold in only her sweater. She was easing herself down from the eave when she felt hands on her waist.

"I'll help you the rest of the way," Warner said.

When she firmly planted her feet on the ground, Warner's hands still rested on her hips. She stepped forward and gave him the kiss she'd been holding back for the past few days. Their lips met in a sweet, soft caress. The electricity between them practically sparked, but the kiss was much too brief as Warner pulled away.

"But you're engaged." Warner's eyes flared with a mix of pain and anger, but he didn't let go of her.

Stella laughed and looked down at the piece of jewelry. "The reason I'm wearing a too-large diamond on a too-tight ring is that I tried on my mother's engagement ring. I didn't have time to lubricate and work it off before the car accident."

"You're not engaged?"

Her lips quirked. "I'm not engaged."

A smile spread across his face as his eyes sparkled. He tugged her to him and wrapped her in a fierce hug.

When he leaned in for another kiss, Stella returned melted into him and surrendered her heart to the moment. Around them, plump, soft snow drifted down from the afternoon sky.

CHAPTER 10

The next morning, Stella arranged to host lunch with the Orion's at her parents' house. Bandit kept on her heels, sensing her excitement.

Yesterday, after the police carted away the Grinch Brothers and she'd thanked Pole again, she'd been exhausted. She exchanged numbers with Warner, and Pole gave her a ride home. Deciding to check on her car tomorrow, she'd showered and went to bed. The next morning, she'd texted Warner to invite them for lunch.

When Warner texted to ask what they could bring, she replied with *egg nog*.

For their group lunch, she cooked chicken cordon bleu with a side of green beans. Since the snickerdoodle cookies had been preserved and uneaten during her absence, they would be for dessert.

She wanted to show the family her gratitude and how special they'd made her feel during their holiday. She'd bonded with all of them after only a few short days.

By the time the doorbell rang, she had festive placemats with poinsettias on the table and a centerpiece of holly glowing with red LED lights. When she opened the door, they all greeted her—Lizzy, Louise, Ralph, and Warner. Ralph held a bottle of wine, and Louise had a round dish Stella suspected was a pie.

"Come in! Come in! I'm so glad you came."

Lizzy bolted across the threshold to Stella and gave a brief hug before kneeling to play with Bandit. She took her shoes off at the door before following the boisterous puppy into the living room.

"We'll put these in the kitchen." Louise and Ralph walked past her, also leaving their shoes by the door.

Stella locked eyes with Warner as her heart skittered a few beats.

He stepped inside and closed the door. "Hi."

She tucked her hands in the pockets of her blue jeans, bunching the bottom hem of her pale green sweater. "Hello. I'm Stella Maddox. I'm thirty-two. I teach survival training to corporate employees and medical missionaries going overseas or south of the border. I proudly served in the Army for six years. After a meniscal tear my fourth year in, I continued to work in communications. Following the Army, I earned my master's degree in education. I have one brother, and my parents own this house. They are currently traveling on vacation."

Warner smiled broadly, took a step closer, and glanced above her. "I'm Warner Orion, and you already know about me and my family. I want to learn all about you, Stella, but first, I'm going to back you up three paces and kiss you senseless under the mistletoe."

Her heart turned light as a feather. "I might have

intentionally placed that there this morning in hopes you might." Her words came out slightly breathless.

He wrapped his arms around her and held nothing back. The kiss was deep and sensual and everything she'd imagined it would be. She melted into the bliss of passion.

When at last they broke away, he asked, "Do you have plans for New Years?" He kept his arms around her.

"No, but I'm open to crashing yours."

He chuckled. "You are welcome to crash any of my holidays. Besides," he looked toward his family gathering at the table, "I don't think you crashed Christmas... I think you saved it."

"You saved me. If you hadn't had a family star-spirit working miracles, I never would have made it safely to your cabin."

"Since we've established that we rescued each other, I'm going to savor this moment a little longer." He leaned in for another kiss.

12 MONTHS LATER

WARNER AND STELLA sat on the sofa in front of the cabin fire. Lizzy was in bed for the night after a day of sledding and snowball fights. She had taken some time to wind down, given her anticipation of Santa coming tonight. Bandit slept at the foot of her bed.

Warner had rented the same cabin from a year ago—the same cabin where 'Star' had shown up on his sofa. He'd brought gifts for Lizzy to open in the morning, though none of them would top the woman and puppy who'd arrived into their lives a year ago.

He and Stella had taken time since last Christmas to date and get know each other better. Stella traveled frequently with her job, but she'd been able to spend a lot of time with him and Lizzy in between. They hiked, skied, zip-lined, camped outdoors, and camped in their own homes. He would never take his second chance at love for granted.

In front of the crackling cabin fire, he turned toward Stella. "One year ago tonight, you found your way to my cabin." Warner was still astounded when he considered the miracle of the family's Christmas Spirit leading Stella to them. "And my heart," he added, looking into those star-lit blue eyes. "And you came back when you didn't have to. You'll forever be the amazing woman I love."

Withdrawing a small box from his pocket, he slipped down onto one knee. He could have asked her to marry him after the first time they'd kissed—and not just because she saved his family from a terrible fate. He'd fallen in love with her within days, but rational behavior prevailed, and he'd given her time to know him and his daughter better.

He opened the box to reveal a diamond ring. "Marry me, Stella. My family's star may have brought you to me, but you're the star that holds my heart."

She smiled with eyes glistening like tinsel on a tree. "Yes. Of course, yes."

As he slipped the ring on her finger, chest bursting with joy, she pulled him to her for a long, slow kiss.

<<<>>>

BRIEF NOTE FROM THE AUTHOR

I HOPE you enjoyed my Christmas Collection. Join my newsletter to learn about my different series and new releases.

MORE ROMANCING THE SPIRIT NOVELLAS
IN BOXED SETS

ROMANCING THE SPIRIT SERIES #1
  Sadie's Spirit / Willow's Windfall
  Cassie's Chase / Phoebe's Pharaoh
  Vanessa's Valentine / Autumn's Angel
  Romancing the Spirit Series #2
  Carol's Christmas / Allison's Alibi
  Gracelynn's Genie / Michelle's Miracle
  Heather's Hero / Chloe's Cupid
  Romancing the Spirit Series #3
  Sabrina's Storm / Jenny's Justice
  Stella's Star / Gigi's Gift
  Phoenix's Phantom / Fiona's Freedom

DEAR READER

If you enjoyed this book and want to know about future releases by CB Samet you can CLICK HERE (www. cbsamet.com) to sign up for my mailing list! I promise I won't spam you. I only send an email when I have a new book released, giveaways, or special discounts. And I'll never sell your information. You can also unsubscribe at any time.

You can also follow me on BookBub.

If you like the concept of ghosts bringing people together in a romantic suspense format, there are many more novellas in the Romancing the Spirit Series in individual books and box sets.

Also, as an author, I rely heavily on readers to spread the word about books they've read. If you enjoyed this story, kindly let others know by posing a brief comment on social media or leave a review where you purchased it.

Thank you for reading,
CB Samet

OTHER BOOKS BY CB SAMET

Looking for more romantic suspense? How about with a Norse Mythology twist? Check out The Shadow Guardians trilogy.

Raven's Flight, a prequel novella

Raine Down, Book 1

Rosalyn's Run, novella

Storm Surge, Book 2

Anka's Orb, novella

Sky Fall, Book 3

Meridian File / Masters File / Box Set 1

McMillan File / Maltisse File /Box Set 2

Storm File / Sullivan File / Box Set 3

Sharp File / Sizani File / Box Set 4

Rivera File / Rucker File / Box Set 5

Richmond File / Redwood File / Box Set 6

Atlas File / Angel File / Box Set 7

Rider Novellas:

Cabrera File / Connor File

Cassidy File / Christmas File

Buy all four!

The Dr. Whyte Adventure Novels

Thriller Series

Black Gold

Whyte Knight

Gray Horizon

Love action/adventure and strong female leads in a fantasy world? Check out my other genre:

The Avant Champion Fantasy Series

The Avant Champion: Rising

Malakai: An Avant Champion Origin of Malos Story (prequel)

The Avant Champion: Honor

The Avant Champion: Ashes

Brothers' Bond: An Avant Champion Malakai Story

The Avant Champion: Conquest

Isabel: An Avant Champion novelette

The Avant Champion: Redeem

www.ingramcontent.com/pod-product-compliance
Lightning Source LLC
Chambersburg PA
CBHW061321190726
48288CB00002B/602